WE WERE
YOUNG ONCE...

THOMAS J. NICHOLS

We Were Young Once...

(Defiance Press & Publishing, LLC)

Printed in the United States of America

10 9 8 7 6 5 4 3 2 1

ISBN-13: 978-1-948035-62-0 (Paperback)
ISBN-13: 978-1-948035-64-4 (eBook)

Edited by Janet Musick
Cover designed by Spomenka Bojanic
Interior designed by Debbi Stocco

Published by Defiance Press and Publishing, LLC

Bulk orders of this book may be obtained by contacting Defiance Press and Publishing, LLC at: www.defiancepress.com.

Public Relations Dept. – Defiance Press & Publishing, LLC
281-581-9300
pr@defiancepress.com

Defiance Press & Publishing, LLC
281-581-9300
info@defiancepress.com

CHAPTER ONE

M y name is Enrique Basurto. This is my story—the ups and the downs, and especially about my Thursdays.

I was raised in a little place you probably never heard of, Hachita, New Mexico. The last census showed us to have a population of forty-nine, but we've shrunk since then. We have a zip code, 88040. That means something to us.

My mom, Sophie, raised my sister, Lupe, and me by herself. Our dad died in an accident in the copper mine in Bisbee, so Mom did what moms do; she raised her kids alone. My parents were married a few years after high school. They were in love, but smart. They waited until they had jobs and some savings before they tied the knot. Lupe was born three years later, and they had me two years after that.

Our perfect little world crashed down on us when I was three years old. Dad was a tire changer on the 400-ton rigs at the open-pit mine. It was one of those freak accidents that just happen. The rig tilted and Dad was crushed. I'll always remember it. We lived in Naco, a few miles south of Bisbee. Two men from the mine came to the house on a Thursday night and told us about it. They were nice and said all the right things, then they were gone. It's as clear as if it was yesterday. Mom got us ready for bed, and then we got on our knees and said our prayers…and cried.

A couple months later, Mom moved us to her parents' old farm in New Mexico. We didn't actually live *in* Hachita but on two acres about a mile northeast of town. We kept a garden with some tomatoes, corn, chilies, plus a few chickens and pigeons. I was five years old when I learned to kill and clean the birds for dinner. I liked the pigeons best 'cause the chickens would scratch and peck me when I tried to wring their necks. The pigeons were easy—just pop their heads off. They cooked up juicy and tender, especially with some jalapenos and corn.

We kept an old Holstein for a while. She had been in a dairy in Las Cruces, but got too old and low on production, so they sold her to us. Wanda, as we called her, was a good cow for a family. We sold a lot of milk from her for about a year, but she was snake-bitten one night on her nose. When we got up in the morning, she was dead: suffocated. Her nose looked like she had a softball stuck up each nostril.

That was my life as a little kid.

* * *

I graduated from Animas High School, and two months later I was in Marine Corps boot camp in San Diego. I gave the Marines six years of my life. It was a time I'll always remember—from

Receiving Barracks to Camp Pendleton and around the world, from combat utility uniforms to dress blues, from being a slick-sleeve recruit to a three-striper. It was burned into my heart and soul. My blood ran Marine green. They were good years in spite of the death and destruction that was dumped on us, which we returned with overwhelming shock and awe. In those few years, I saw more of the world than ever before, including Afghanistan, a place I never want to see again.

I did two combat tours and lost a good friend to an IED. It was on a Thursday afternoon and we were almost back to the firebase when we were hit. Bobby was in the tactical vehicle behind mine. I don't know how we didn't get hit, but that's the way war was. Luck. Pure and simple luck. It had nothing to do with how good or how screwed up you were, how tough or how wimpy you were. You're in the right or wrong place at just the right or wrong time. It's a hard lesson to swallow, but it's the truth.

By God's good graces, I came through without a scratch. I earned a two-year degree from Cal State-Fullerton through Internet classes and was looking forward to a career in the Corps. However, at the end of my second tour, I shipped back to Pendleton and called it quits. I liked being a Marine and planned to stay as long as they would have me. But life's lessons never end. The years and stress of being a single parent had not been kind to Mom. Lupe was married, lived in Denver and almost never got home, and I was on another planet. The decision was hard but necessary. I only had one mom.

On Monday, I was a Sergeant E-5 with my unit at Las Pulgas on Basilone Road in Pendleton. Tuesday I was a civilian, Greyhound-bound to Lordsburg, New Mexico.

* * *

I joked to myself. A job in Hachita? It didn't exist. Nevertheless, I checked the Internet, went to the employment offices in Lordsburg and Deming, and came to a stark conclusion: I was unemployed.

I had heard it said before, and it was true. Good fortune falls to those who keep their noses to the grindstone. I was in the general store in Animas and ran into a state trooper, a black guy. He listened to me bitch about not having a job. We talked a while about being a cop and, as though he'd memorized it, the words of Dr. Martin Luther King rolled off his tongue, "If you can't fly, then run; if you can't run, then walk; if you can't walk, then crawl; but whatever you do, you have to keep moving forward."

I looked at him. He was squared away and had his shit together…even if he was at the end of the world on the Mexican border. We finished our coffee and he paid the tab with a smile, "There ain't no free lunch."

* * *

After a twenty-six-week training course, I graduated from the Department of Public Safety Academy. That was followed by a three-month field-training period in the Las Cruces Patrol Division. When my training was over, instead of going on highway patrol, they assigned me back to the Academy to study Human and Drug Interdiction and Prosecution. From there, it was on to the Drug Enforcement Agency (DEA) eighty-hour course in Arizona—not bad duty, staying at a four-star hotel in Scottsdale while studying link analysis, trap and trace devices, undercover techniques, mail cover, inter-agency cooperation, asset forfeiture, and the list goes on.

There was some irony to this. I had never considered being a cop, but life doesn't always play out according to our own whims. Being a "lifer" in the Corps was simply not going to be.

Nevertheless, I vaguely remembered many years ago hearing about Mom's Uncle Tony in Arizona. He was an undercover cop who was murdered. I didn't recall anything about his story. Mom never talked about it but still, the memory was there. I never asked her about him nor did she discuss it.

* * *

After almost a year of criminal justice schools, I packed my suitcases into my new-to-me GMC pickup and drove home to Hachita. Mom had given up her job at the Antelope Wells border crossing where she cleaned the buildings and laundered the officers' uniforms for some extra money. Now she took care of the garden and a few chickens. She had given up on the pigeons. They ate more than they were worth.

I had a week's vacation coming, so put it to good use cleaning up the place. It was home to us—a *good* home with two bedrooms, a bathroom, and a great room that served as the kitchen, dining room and living room. It was about a thousand square feet, a flat-roofed adobe with a swamp box on the roof. Mom had built turquoise painted wooden flower boxes under the bedroom windows, and my old high school friends and I built a covered front deck and topped it off with a porch swing.

We kept about a dozen Leghorn hens in their coop behind the house. Our water well was beyond the coop, which meant there was always plenty of fresh water for the house, the hens, and for a yard. Mom kept a meticulous little lawn between the house and the chain link fence we used to keep out the occasional stray livestock.

Sometimes we had a rattlesnake around the coop, but most of the time they weren't a problem; they were good for rats and mice. That's why we didn't chase off the roadrunners that scurried around the pen. They killed the snakes, so Mother Nature did a balancing act for us.

* * *

Mom was fifty years old but looked much older. Her fingers were twisted with arthritis and her knees snapped and popped when she walked. Life had been tough on her.

We went to Sunday Mass in Columbus because our church in Hachita had closed, then ate lunch at Pepe's Café—*huevos, papas, frijoles, tortillas, y chocolate caliente.* On the way home, I pulled a letter out of my shirt pocket and handed it to her. "A note from *El Patron,*" I said. "He gave me an assignment I think you'll like."

"Que pasa, hijo?" she asked when she pulled the single sheet from the envelope.

I kept my eyes on the road, glancing at her as she read my orders. She wet her lips, then slowly allowed herself a wisp of a smile. She looked directly at me. Her eyes danced. "Ricky, you'll be working right here almost in our front yard?"

"Seguro que si. I'll take care of my Momma." I pressed my knees against the steering wheel and cupped my hands together

like the advertisement on TV. "You're in good hands with Ricky."

She squealed, and tears coursed down her cheeks. "My little boy went to the Marines, but now you're home. No longer *mi hijo, pero el hombre de la casa*." Seconds later, she pursed her lips and shook her head ever so slightly. Her eyes were unblinking as she looked straight out the windshield when she spoke. It was like a Marine sniper with that one-thousand-yard stare. "Listen to me. Be careful out there. I don't want anything to happen to you." She didn't say anything else on the ride home, but her eyes told me she was a million miles away.

* * *

The Multi-Agency Human and Controlled Substance Interdiction Task Force was a new working group consisting of DPS, DEA, ICE, Border Patrol (BP), and deputies from Luna and Dona Ana Counties Sheriff's Departments. The Border Patrol was the agency-in-charge, and their supervisory agent was a carrot-top, freckle-faced Mexican who joked that there was a *huero* in the woodpile somewhere. Nevertheless, Miguel O'Rourke was as Mexican as a person could be. He wasn't exactly our GQ model, but more like a Salvation Army customer—comfortable and casual.

Our twelve-member unit was an eclectic group of law enforcement and military veterans. Also, what we had in common was we had lived close to the border somewhere between Tucson and Laredo, were fluent in Spanish, and to some degree with the various dialects spoken in Central and/or South America. We weren't clock watchers—just the opposite. We were committed to our mission.

Our headquarters was a converted ranch house in the middle of five acres of desert on New Mexico State Highway 9 west of Columbus, and just north of the International Boundary. It stuck out like a sore thumb with a ten-foot-high, chain-link fence topped with concertina wire, light stanchions around the perimeter, a forty-foot radio tower, and a holding pen with an authorized capacity of twenty males, ten females, and five family units. It wasn't fancy, but served as a Task Force office and gave the BP a short-term holding area for detainees.

Our radio command center was at the Customs and Border Protection Station on Hwy. 11 in Columbus. It was here that New Mexico 11 changed into Chihuahua Mexico Highway 2. It's considered a good border crossing because it doesn't have the crowds of the El Paso/Juarez station.

Going west from Columbus are miles of empty God-forsaken desert until Antelope Wells.

* * *

Something we learned in the Academy was a tired old story—don't be surprised by what surprises you. In my case, it was true. Her name was Rosalinda Marquez.

We went to high school together. She was beautiful with her silky black hair, delicate lips, and always dressed like the queen of the cowgirls—a starched blouse, tight jeans, and cowboy boots. Her warmth and personality tugged at me the first moment I saw her. My soul filled with her spirit. I nicknamed her that exact moment—*Muncie*, because of her rosy red cheeks.

Her elegant parents, heirs to a land grant from the Gadsden

Purchase era, were owners of a massive cattle operation. Raising their daughters, Rosalinda and Victoria, to carry on their heritage in body and soul was of the utmost importance to them—graceful, personable, and modest.

Rosalinda and I dated through high school but, after graduation, the combination of time and distance drew us apart. Then, after all those years, with no forewarning, there she was…magnificent as ever. I was off-duty out clubbing in Las Cruces with a couple of buddies. We had steaks, and ended the evening at the Club Guadalajara. It was perfect timing, but I'll never understand how it came to pass. It was as though an angel told her to look up the moment we paid our cover charge and entered the bar. Our eyes met. I froze, and she did, too. She was in a booth with a couple of girlfriends eating chips and chatting away. Our eyes locked onto each other. A wisp of a smile formed on her lips. My heart raced. I stepped around my friends and moved in her direction as she scooted out of the booth. We reached out to one another. Our fingers touched for the briefest moment before I pulled her to me. A chill ran down my back. She chuckled lightly and pressed closer to me.

"Ricky, I remember you'd never ask me to dance, but you'd ask me to shine your belt buckle," she said with a light, closed-fist jab to my chest. She leaned back with my hands around her waist and her soft hands around my neck. "All you cowboys thought you had to wear those huge belt buckles."

I shrugged off her comment and whispered, "Rosalinda, so many years, but now…" My voice trailed.

She leaned in, kissed my ear, then looked into my eyes. Her voice was barely above a whisper, "Ricky, I can't believe what is happening. We were about to leave and something told me to just hang loose, so we got another beer and you came sauntering in.

9

That's how you used to walk," she chuckled. "You never walked, you *sauntered*, like 'Here I am.' Truthfully, Ricky, seeing you here is a God thing."

I held her fingers and stepped back to admire her—her hair and cheeks, her precious red lips, a starched white cowgirl shirt, Levi's and, as always, her Old Gringo cowboy boots.

We introduced our friends to each other, then found a corner table just for us. We laughed, talked, and watched our friends dancing and partying. We had another beer and some buffalo wings, then bade adios to our friends and left them to get to know each other. And, too, we had to re-introduce ourselves to each other.

We slipped through the crowd and out to my truck in the parking lot. I pulled up on I-10, bound for the exit a few miles down the highway. We exited the interstate and onto a secondary road leading to Columbus where she lived. I could have listened to her all night as she recapped the after-high school years, the years we had been apart. Her voice was as soft as the brush of an angel's wings.

While I was off to war, Rosalinda went to New Mexico State University where she earned her Bachelor's and Master's degrees in Anthropology. By the time I was out of the Corps and had completed the Police Academy and DEA training, she was a regional supervisor for New Mexico State. Her primary responsibility was to administer their anthropological research sites in the vast emptiness of southern New Mexico, an area with a treasure chest of primitive artifacts in the thornscrub hinterlands of the southwest.

With miles of lonesome desert behind us, we pulled into the parking lot at her condo, appropriately named *Haciendas de 9-11*, not in recognition of the date of infamy, but simply named for the nearby intersection of New Mexico Highways 9 and 11.

I had shared my life's adventures, along with those of my mom and sister. Now the moment was at hand. We were alone with each other. I killed the engine. An El Paso radio station was playing Tejano music: *música al otro lado de la medianoche, música para los amantes solamente.* The moon was full, and the girl of my dreams reached across the console and held my hand.

We sat there until dawn was on the horizon, sharing our souls with each other. Tomorrow, or more accurately, *today* was Sunday. She had the day off, but I was scheduled to be on duty at ten o'clock. If I hurried, I could get a few hours of sleep, so I walked her to the door, shared a good-morning kiss, and slipped onto Hwy. 9 to home.

CHAPTER TWO

Routine is not an accurate word, but the Task Force more or less settled into one. We gave backup to the BP if they were short-handed, which was almost every day. We chased mules and coyotes, found lost and frightened illegal immigrants who were stranded, and hauled bundles of marijuana out of the backcountry to our trucks. The work was hard but satisfying. We knew we were only a little plug in a huge dam, but we did our part and did it well.

Backing up the BP, though, was only a fraction of our work. From our personal lives living along the border, we were suave, grubby, snappy, or bastard enough as the situation demanded to intermingle with populations on either side of the border. From that, it was a slow but steady process of developing a network of informants. None of them were saints because saints weren't in this business. "Sinners," we joked. "That's what we wanted. Lots of 'em." Some did it for the money, others because we put the squeeze on them...pay the piper or do the time. It was that simple.

We caught them and they could work off the charges we held in abeyance or go to jail. Most chose the former.

My first major case came just a few weeks after our unit was organized. We were following up on a tip from one of my snitches. The sun was setting after a long, hot and dry Wednesday. My partner was Chuey Molina. He was over six feet tall and built like a mountain man. We were dressed for the outdoors wearing Levi's, work shirts, straw hats, and boots. Our bullet-resistant vests were tucked behind the seat but readily available. Each of us carried an H&K P2000 double-action .40 caliber pistol and our M4 carbines racked out of sight behind the front seat.

I was driving my undercover pickup, a two-year-old Ford four-wheel drive. We parked on a scrubby knoll beneath a mesquite tree to savor the bit of shade it offered. Chuey scanned the rugged wasteland. It was spotted with creosote bushes and prickly pear cactus, dry washes and ravines, and a few critters—jackrabbits, four-legged coyotes, and an occasional white-tail deer.

The desolate landscape was shrouded with tell-tale clouds of dust rolling on the horizon, evidence of BP trucks towing tractor tires along a path of drag strips in the dry desert soil. That technique was a throwback to the early days of the Texas Rangers. As the primary law enforcers of the west, the Rangers rode the border scanning the ground for tracks of bandits and *tequileros*. Once they had "cut track," the Rangers followed them for however many days it might take to apprehend the thieves and liquor runners.

The modern Border Patrol refreshed the strips almost every day, weather permitting, so follow-up units could spot fresh footprints northbound from the International Boundary and cut track until they ran down the violators—another little cog in the wheel of justice to protect the border.

Chuey froze and leaned into his binoculars. "Got 'em," he whispered. "About five hundred yards south/southwest. Three perps." He caught his breath and wet his lips. "Two carrying bundles. Guy in the rear has a long gun slung over his shoulder."

I grabbed my glasses and followed his line of sight. There they were. Heads bowed under the weight of their loads, trudging in the soft sand of the wash, and keeping below the horizon.

Chuey grabbed the mic from the clip below the dashboard. "Zulu-one," he barked.

"Zulu-one," dispatch replied.

"We're a half-mile south of Hwy. 9, just off the Sandia Road on a knoll. Three perps, possibly armed, and carrying a load, are northbound in Julian Wash. They'll be out of sight in a couple of minutes."

The crackly voice from the helicopter broke in. "Omaha-One, we can be there in about ten minutes."

"10-4," the dispatcher said in her somber, monotone voice.

A BP unit came on the air. "Charlie-4, we're about five miles west. Can be there in a few minutes."

"10-4," she said again.

We knew our plan was to cut them off. Chuey was back on the radio, "Zulu-one," he continued, "we'll be on foot and cut them off from getting back across the border." In a smooth practiced motion, we slipped our vests on, grabbed the rifles, and snapped our radios onto our vests. Ten minutes passed while we huffed and puffed to get into the wash south of the walkers when the radio crackled again. "Charlie-4, on foot and into the wash north of the walkers."

Almost simultaneously, Omaha was on the air. "Ground units, we see your vehicles and the wash. Will come in low for a look-see."

The two of us crept warily north in the deep ravine, the sides rising ten feet over our heads. With weapons at the ready, we scanned every bush and shadow for whomever might lie in wait for us. The chopping sound of the helicopter broke the stillness of the desert and a staccato voice was on the radio. "Got 'em," Omaha yelled. "They ducked into an overhang in the wash. Out of sight, but we know they're in there." There was a pause, then Omaha was back. "Zulu, we have a visual on you. You're about two hundred yards south of where we last saw them."

"Charlie-4, we're still southbound. Got a distance for us?"

"Hold your position," Omaha barked. "You're almost on top of them."

We heard the helicopter PA system bark in Spanish, "Come out slowly. Stay in the ravine. Hands up high and get on your knees." There was a pause, then Omaha came on the radio. "Zulu, one is running to you. No visible weapon or load."

Seconds later, a confused and frightened teenage boy ran straight at us. Our long guns were pointed in his face. He froze and fell to the ground, sniveling in Spanish and English, "*Me rindo.* I surrender. *Me rindo.*"

I patted him down only to find he had wet his pants. I finished the search and flex-cuffed him while Chuey kept watch up the wash. Moments later, Charlie-4 called in. "10-45 with two adults, plus two marijuana bundles and a shotgun. Everything 10-4."

We watched Omaha peel off with a casual, "Omaha 10-8," and disappear into the setting sun.

It was midnight by the time we completed our documentation of Abel Gonzales, his son Emilio, and grandson Felix. We put the juvenile in the holding area, the adults in jail, and the gun and marijuana marked and secured in the evidence locker.

That was the end of my first big case. I didn't realize until I was almost home how nervous and shaken I had been sneaking up on our quarry, not knowing what to expect. It was like war. We had our battle plan but didn't know theirs. It wasn't a good feeling.

Something about this, though, was different. I didn't know whether to believe them or not. Most people we interrogated lied to us. They had nothing to lose. The three of them were a granddad, son, and grandson. Their ages ranged from fourteen to fifty-eight. We separated them for the interviews, but they were consistent with what they said, so consistent that we assumed they were lying and were going to stick to their story: the cartel made them do it. The old man responded best to our inquires, but his grandson was too petrified to talk. He just kept crying.

This wasn't the first time they had carried a load across the desert. They had done it twice before and been paid $100 each when they got back to their home near Los Juguetes, southwest of Palomas. He was believable, but that might be because he told it so much he believed it himself—the cartel paid when the load was delivered, or his family paid the consequences.

Sounds good, I thought, *but it's a bunch of bullshit.*

* * *

Chuey and I met with O'Rourke mid-morning the next day—Thursday morning. We reviewed the case, and I gave him my opinion. All of them were lying. The story was too pat to be trustworthy.

O'Rourke shrugged his shoulders and bounced back and forth in English and Spanish. "We'll see. *Lo comprobaré.* I'll let you know if I find anything out. *Chingado,* get out of here and get to work."

Chuey drove as we pulled out of our secure area. He tucked the seatbelt beneath his butt and squeezed the steering wheel. He grimaced as he made a hard right turn onto Hwy. 9.

"This is a bunch of shit," he bellowed. "We should have just let 'em go. It's not worth it."

I fastened my seatbelt tighter as we roared down the highway. I gripped the dashboard with one hand and twisted around to face my partner. "What the fuck do you mean?"

"I lied to myself all night, and now I know what they said was true. We," he pointed back and forth between us, "got somebody killed last night for a friggin' load of grass."

I raised my voice and fired back. "Don't lay that shit on me. We did our job and, if those fuckers had stayed on their side of the fence, this never would have happened." I took a moment to catch my breath, then continued. "Besides that, even if they told us the truth, it's their problem. Not ours."

Chuey glanced out of the corner of his eye at me. "Keep telling yourself that, ol' buddy. When we find out what the price was, then you tell me how fucking right you were."

He slowed and whipped into a parking spot at the Sinaloa Café in Columbus. His voice was barely discernible when he pushed his door open, got out, and slammed it behind him. "I don't care if it's still morning, I'm going to have a shot and beer to get my head straight before we tackle anymore *mulas*."

The dimly lit bar was dead as a tomb. We were the only customers besides two old men who were slouched over the bar nursing their drinks. The bartender was a thirty-something dark-skinned Latina, dressed to encourage tips. Her skin-tight blouse was open almost to her bellybutton. Her cut-off Levi's barely covered her butt.

"*Que tal, amigos*," she said as we pulled up two more stools to the bar. *"¿Qué gustan tomar?"* I pulled a twenty from my wallet and tossed it on the bar. "Two Jack Blacks and a couple Buds."

Seeing my partner was somewhere between pissed off and ready to blow, the sexy bartender didn't attempt small talk; instead, she busied herself at the far end of the bar washing and drying glasses.

Chuey sipped his shot of whiskey, then glanced at me with a smart-ass grin and threw the shot down his throat. *"Tenemos trabajo que hacer, amigo.* Let's get to work," he blurted. He chugged his frosty beer in the same manner and shrugged his shoulders. "Their fault, not ours? Right?"

I returned his shrug. "Who gives a crap? We do our jobs and the chips fall where they may." I shook my head and continued, "We don't make the friggin' rules; we just do our jobs." I tossed my shot down and followed it with the beer in one long swallow. I slammed the mug down with a belly-killing belch and looked Chuey in the eye. "God didn't make us to save the world all by ourselves. We do our jobs, do them well, maintain our ethics, and from that, *que sera, sera.*" I paused but cut him off when he opened his mouth to speak. "That's what we signed on for and that's what we're going to do. 10-4?"

He held his hands up in surrender and a half-hearted chuckle. "Hey, amigo. I'm your friend, remember?" He looked down at the floor, then back at me. He was dead serious, nodding his head. "Yeah, we do our jobs and keep our noses clean. There's nothing wrong with that." He stood up and stretched. "It's just that I think the world is screwed up and we got dumped on the front lines and are supposed to fix it."

I laughed and got up. "That's how we felt in Afghanistan, too."

* * *

We left the bar, zipped into the drive-thru at Jimmy John's, and bought sandwiches for lunch. We already had stowed a five-gallon water cooler and three one-quart containers under a tarp in the back. They were for us, plus we had enough for any dehydrated illegals we might encounter.

Now Chuey was his old self. A couple of miles west of town he pulled off the blacktop, through the ditch, and took a short-cut across a patch of desert where we could perch on a knoll and watch the fence line.

There wasn't anything wrong, but I felt something in my bones. It told me this wasn't going to be a good day. It was more than intuition. It was like God himself was talking to us.

The hours passed infinitesimally slow as they usually did on Thursdays—the same day every week it seemed everybody had taken a siesta. The desert was still and quiet. Not a breath of wind floated over the countryside. It was as if the whole world was at peace. I watched the last rays of sunlight disappear over the western mountaintops. Our workday was almost over and we had survived. I checked my watch—almost seven o'clock. We had backed up a state trooper on a traffic stop on Hwy. 9 that turned out to be nothing special, jumped a battery for one of our units in the headquarters parking lot, and did a few random checks on areas we knew were popular with border crossers. It was a nothing day and we were ready to call it quits until *it* happened.

The call came over the radio. It wasn't God, but it *was* Miguel O'Rourke, "10-38 office." We looked at each other. Bosses don't call at the end of a shift to tell you good news.

CHAPTER THREE

O'Rourke's desk was a jumble of bureaucratic forms, scratch-pads, coffee stains, and a computer. It was a mess, but fit his mood perfectly.

Chuey and I each pulled up a straight-backed chair to his desk. He leaned back in his faux leather secretary chair, crossed his arms across his chest, and glared. His voice was crisp. "You did every-thing right, so don't second-guess yesterday." He paused, let out a strong exhale, and pursed his lips. "What happened, happened. We do our job and let the chips fall where they may. End of story."

"Stop screwing with us," Chuey snapped. His emotions were scrawled across his face. "Give it to us straight."

O'Rourke leaned forward angrily, hands pressed flat on the desk, blood vessels in his face about to burst. His breath smelled of burnt coffee. "They beat the shit out of the grandmother and mother, and took the twelve-year-old girl, Catalina, with them."

Chuey sagged in his chair. His voice was barely audible, his face downcast, but his eyes glared at O'Rourke. "I knew it. I knew it. We should've let them go."

"That's bullshit," O'Rourke fired back. "You had no way of knowing anything ahead of time. You did your job and did it well. Other than that…" his voice softened, "shit happens." He leaned back again, picked up his dirty cup, and sipped the last drops of his cold coffee.

He had his say and was done with it.

Chuey stood up slowly. His shoulders stooped. He looked like a tired old man, eyes downcast to the floor and his feet shuffling as he turned to leave. "I'm done," he said, then went outside, got into his truck and left.

I started after him, but O'Rourke called me back. "Let him go. He's going to have to work this out one way or the other." He cocked his head and gave me a shit-eating grin. "Go home. Go see your girlfriend. Do something worthwhile and then get some sleep. We'll talk tomorrow."

* * *

Rosalinda and I sat across from each other at her kitchen table, each of us nursing a double shot of *Anejo* Tequila. I was wearing my sweat-stained clothes and boots from a day in the desert. Rosalinda was fresh and clean, wearing a pink-and-white flowered blouse and tan shorts. She was barefooted.

From outward appearances, we couldn't be more different, but the outer shell can be misleading—we were in love.

The room was dark but for a light over the stove and music drifting in from the living room. She reached out and took my hand. A single tear clung to her eye. "I'm so sorry, Ricky. Is there anything I can do?" She shook her head faintly as the tear broke loose and dripped down her cheek. "Don't let it take you down. Yes, it's horrible, but there's nothing you or Chuey could have done that would have changed any of it. The world is an evil place and whether it was the two of you or someone else, it was going to happen. Sooner or later, but the die was cast. There was nothing you could do to alter the outcome."

She pushed back and went to the cabinet, got the bottle of *Anejo*, and topped off our glasses. Taking her seat, her lips curled into a gentle smile. She hoisted her glass in a toast, "To the guy I love, and may God in heaven lift this millstone from his shoulders."

I toasted her back, lifting the glass with my grubby, dirty hands. "Love bears it out, even to the edge of doom," I said, then lowered the drink to the table. "Not quite Shakespeare, but as close as I'm going to get." Tears came without warning and poured down my cheeks. I gasped for breath and wiped my face with my bare hands. "Sorry, Muncie. It's been a shitty day, but I want to say this with all my heart." I couldn't breathe. My body quivered as I struggled to regain my composure. Taking another deep breath, I reached for her hands. We looked at each other, eye to eye, then I blurted it out, "I want to marry you."

Rosalinda rose slowly from the chair. Her eyes pierced the depths of my soul. She moved as effortlessly as a spirit when she stepped around the table and leaned down. I don't know whether it was a second or an hour before she pressed her lips to mine— a kiss like no other, then cupped my face in her soft hands. "*Te amaré para siempre.*"

It wouldn't have made any difference if it had been spoken in a million different languages. The tenderness of her voice, the softness of her lips, and the sparkle in her eyes would have pierced any man's soul. Love is not bound by language.

I took her hand and led her to the living room, pulling her down beside me on the couch.

There wasn't a fireplace in her apartment, but there was a flat-screen TV showing a video of a roaring fireplace. To us, that was as good as it was going to get. We held each other close and kissed, then explored the bounds of our passion.

The fireplace never went out before we fell asleep.

* * *

I pulled in the driveway at the crack of dawn. My mom was wearing her nightgown and dragging the hose to put the sprinkler on the grass. "*Buenos dias, hijo,*" she said. "Did you have a hard night?"

I laughed when I climbed out of the truck. "Momma, you're not going to believe this, but Muncie and I are getting married."

She dropped the hose, which immediately slung around like a chicken with its head cut off, squirting her feet and slippers with cold water. She screamed and laughed as she jumped free from the freezing spray. "*Hijo,* I love you. I'm so happy." She ran to me, wrapping me in her arms and kissing my cheek. "Ricky, I'm so proud of you and proud *for* you. And I love your Muncie like she is my own daughter."

* * *

It was noon when I got to our headquarters and noticed Chuey's truck wasn't in the parking lot. I went inside, stopped by the snack bar and picked up a cup of hot chocolate, then went to O'Rourke's office. I found him with his face buried in the computer screen. I shut the door with a solid thud to be sure I got his attention, then pulled up a chair across from him. He leaned back and turned toward me.

My voice quivered with anger and frustration. "Chuey?" I asked. "What's up?"

O'Rourke's expression was stoic. "He's not coming back. Agent Molina turned everything in at the El Paso office. He's gone." Miguel lifted his stained cup, turned around to his ever-present Mr. Coffee, and poured himself another.

He didn't offer one to me before he continued his monologue, shaking his head in displeasure. "The El Paso Agent-in-Charge, Freddy Gomez, sent me an email. Molina wanted to quit, but they refused and put him on paid leave. It has a technical term—compassion fatigue."

Miguel twisted his lips and shrugged. "What happened to the women was too much to cope with. He cratered. Gomez didn't say anything other than that, and I didn't ask any questions." He turned his back, put his cup on the credenza, and spoke without facing me. "As I said, shit happens."

I nodded to the back of his head, scooted my chair away, and went to the truck. There was work to do, and it started with the Gonzales family.

* * *

I checked records and found staff from Texas Social Services as well as from Customs and Immigration had notified them of the situation in Los Juguetes. On the bright side, ICE had already begun the legal process to offer asylum to the mother and grandmother. It was going to be a little more complicated with the two men. They faced felony charges at the state and federal level.

Felix, the fourteen-year-old, was in the juvenile center in Las Cruces. He would be released eventually, but the adults' matters needed to be resolved first.

It was three o'clock in the afternoon when I found Abel and Emilio in the El Paso Detention Center. We met in a compact, sterile interrogation room consisting of a solid wooden table bolted to the floor, three straight-backed chairs, and a glaring overhead light. It was designed to be uncomfortable, and it was. This wasn't a place for chit-chat, but it also wasn't a comfortable place to discuss the life-and-death issues they faced with felony charges, their spouses being beaten nearly to death, and the little girl in the hands of the cartel.

A gray-uniformed security officer escorted them down the hall. Each was dressed in a standard pink pullover shirt and similarly colored drawstring pants with shower shoes on their feet. They weren't handcuffed, but looked exhausted and mentally fatigued—unshaven, stoop-shouldered, and struggling to make the next step.

Conscious of the need to be professional yet sympathetic for their situation, I offered a perfunctory smile and gestured to them to be seated. Abel returned a forced smile and nodded politely when we made eye contact. Emilio didn't acknowledge me. He simply scooted the chair up, sat down with his hands folded on his lap and his head down.

Even though they had my business card from when they were booked, I introduced myself in as gentle a voice as I could muster.

"Recuerdo," Abel said, and so began our conversation. Both men spoke halting English, so we conversed in Spanish. They had already been in contact with an Immigration attorney who would also represent them in the criminal matters they faced.

They spoke in generalities, but it quickly came to the forefront that they couldn't speak in any detail until their attorney was present. Nevertheless, Abel indicated they would like to work with us in order to minimize the consequences they faced while at the same time finding Catalina and reuniting their family.

I acknowledged their concerns and offered them my cellphone. Abel nodded appreciation and took the phone. He pulled the business card of Adolph Mungia, Attorney-at-Law, from his pocket. Moments later, the two men had a brief conversation. Abel gave several affirmative nods of his head, then clicked off. He gave the slightest hint of a smile.

"He'll be here in twenty minutes," he said, gesturing back and forth between the three of us.

We spoke briefly about Catalina, then I excused myself and went to the visitors' waiting area. I called O'Rourke on my cellphone. He answered on the second ring.

"¿Que pasa?" he asked.

We were discussing the terms of negotiating a deal with the Gonzales family when a well-dressed Hispanic man in his thirties entered from the parking lot. He wore a blue blazer and tan pants with his dark hair combed straight back. A red, white, and green Mexican flag pin adorned the lapel on his coat. We caught each other's eyes when he started across the room, then turned in my direction and spoke. "Agent Basurto?"

Clicking off my phone, I answered, "Yes, sir."

We introduced ourselves and shook hands. Mungia gestured toward a room marked *Attorney's Conference.* "Shall we?" he asked as he started toward the door with me following a few steps behind.

The interview room was similar to the prisoner interrogation room except the table was not bolted to the floor. We took our seats, exchanged professional chit-chat for a moment, then turned to the business at hand.

"Will you help my clients find a reasonable way out of the quandary in which they find themselves?" he asked.

I leaned forward on the desk and nodded affirmatively. "Work with us and you'll find it a two-way street. If they play games, they'll do hard time in La Tuna. It's as simple as that."

"My clients will give you the Salinas brothers' heads on a platter."

My interest was tweaked. I had never heard of the Salinas family.

Both of us sat back and smiled. It was a deal. Another hour passed before we finalized our negotiations. Abel and Emilio would accept a misdemeanor plea for possession of marijuana, we would dismiss the weapons charge, and their jail sentence would be counted as "time served."

Their part of the deal was they would give us everything they knew about the drug and human trafficking in the Juarez/Palomas district, and the Sinaloa/La Linea Cartel. If everything worked out as planned, the men and their wives would be offered asylum. Additionally, they would be assisted in obtaining reasonable housing, medical service, and education. Also, their son would be released with no criminal or juvenile history in his background.

If everything culminated as planned, the Gonzaleses would have good lives north of the border. The land of milk and honey would be theirs.

Maybe.

WE WERE YOUNG ONCE...

An hour later, I was having coffee with O'Rourke in his office. The deal was done. The ball was in my court. I would be the lead agent in Operation Catalina—rescue or recover the little girl, and arrest anyone involved in the human and drug trafficking.

CHAPTER FOUR

C huey was still on leave, so seven-year DEA veteran Anna Fernandez was transferred from the Las Cruces office to become my new partner. We were introduced to each other in O'Rourke's office. Agent Fernandez was a comely thirty-something but dressed for the outdoors—khaki shirt, tan cargo trousers, and Hi-Tec hiking boots. We exchanged business formalities, and then the two of us adjourned to the *Roca Alta* Café in Columbus for a breakfast of *machaca chimichangas* and coffee.

We hit it off immediately. She had served four years in the Corps, which included fourteen months in the Middle East as a Hazardous Duty Demolition instructor or, as she put it, "Teaching young Marines to render harmless an IED and keep all their fingers at the same time."

Her sense of humor and commitment to our battle with drug and sex traffickers struck me perfectly. She had twice received commendations for her work in the El Paso-to-Santa Fe I-25 pipeline running drugs and sex offenders northbound toward the greater Denver area.

She was married to a chiropractor and was the mother of a two-year-old boy, and the family had moved recently to Las Cruces, so this assignment fit her perfectly.

Anna listened intently to my telling of the Wednesday evening marijuana bust, the three generations of Gonzaleses, and the after-effect it had on the family. Anna was particularly taken aback by the kidnapping of twelve-year-old Catalina. She stopped in the middle of a bite and sat back in her chair. Her eyes were piercing. "Tell me what you've done to find her."

For the briefest moment, I thought she was challenging me, a rookie. My response was slow and measured. "It's a bifurcated but related response for the two issues—rescue or recover the child..."

She cut me off, leaning forward, raising her hand, and shaking her head. "Aren't they the same?"

"Not at all," I fired back. "Our goal is to get her out alive but, if that fails, we continue until we recover her remains—rescue alive; recover dead."

Anna sat back slowly. "My apologies. Of course, you're right. Rescue or recover is our primary goal, and the drug deal is secondary."

"Yep," I replied. "Dead or alive, we see this through."

Her eyes were downcast as she sipped the last of her drink. She spoke softly. "I truly am sorry, Enrique, for speaking out so forcefully. I should have heard you through."

I gestured with a shrug of my shoulders, "*Que sera, sera,*" finished my coffee, and scooted my chair back. "We've got work to do."

Anna immersed herself in making a phone call as we walked back to my truck. She obviously was familiar with the person she was speaking to. It was about the Gonzales women—Elise the grandmother and Abril, Catalina's mother. They went back and forth in Spanish to each other for a few minutes before Anna gave a polite chortle and bade a polite, *"Que te vaya buen, Hermana."*

I got behind the wheel as Anna slipped into the passenger seat and tucked the phone into her leg pocket. She leaned back with a strong exhale.

"Wow, that was big. I didn't know if they would do it, but the nuns at the San Albino Basilica in Mesilla offered temporary housing for the women." She paused and twisted her lips. "They're not too sure about Felix; maybe yes, maybe no. We'll have to wait and see."

"Good," I replied. "At least we have a rough outline for a game plan."

I pulled onto the boulevard, turned south toward the crossing at Palomas, and wormed my way into the traffic. "Let's start with Catalina. I have a trustworthy contact, Sergeant Sergio Mora with the Chihuahua State Police."

Anna adjusted her seatbelt and looked at me with a question mark scrawled across her face, "How do you define trustworthy?"

"His brother was killed by the cartel in an ambush last year. I met him through a mutual acquaintance and we meshed pretty quickly." I nodded my head, convincing myself we could trust our Mexican colleague. "He's done a few deals with our mutual associate, and he gave me a tip last week about a load house. I passed it on to DEA and they took it down. It was a dumpy little house in Silver City, but they seized twenty kilos of cocaine and busted an old man who was sitting on it. He was just some *pobrecito* the cartel put the squeeze on. They paid him a few hundred bucks to keep it in his house until they were ready to move it."

I shrugged my shoulders, irritated at how the little guy was consistently screwed. "But, that's life. He takes the fall and the world keeps on spinning."

"Where does that leave us?" Anna asked.

"We cross the border and meet with Sgt. Mora. It's like a grade-B movie, but it works. We're a couple doing some shopping. Act normal. Hold hands, laugh, and have a good time." I chuckled at the make-believe world we worked in—pretend you're not pretending when you *are* pretending. "We'll stop in Fernando's Hideaway for a beer. Mora's dad owns the place. If everything is cool, he'll call a cab for us—not just any cab. It's part of their organization. From there, we go to a house on the south side of town. That's where we'll meet with Sergio."

Anna frowned. "This *does* sound like a Hollywood script."

I gave a Cheshire cat grin back at her, "But it works. Wait and see."

Forty-five minutes later, we strode hand in hand through the plaza, sipped bottled soft drinks and enjoyed a Mariachi band in the center of the square. I bought a pack of Chiclets from a street vendor, then guided my *girlfriend* into the bar. We found a corner table, shifted the chairs around, and took our seats facing the front door and the bar.

Moments later, a middle-aged man, his dark hair greased back and wearing an apron over his soiled white shirt approached. He wiped the table off, then gave a slight nod and smiled. "The usual?" he asked.

"*Seguro*," I replied.

He leaned down to me and spoke in Spanish. "It'll be a few minutes. I'll get you a beer. *Negro Modelo*, right?"

He looked at Anna, "And for the lady?"

She smiled. "Modelo for me, too. "

He turned toward the bar, calling out the drink order to the bartender. *"Dos Negros,* Mario.*"*

Two beers each and thirty minutes later, Fernando picked up the empty bottles, cleaned the table, and gave a casual, "Your taxi is ready."

* * *

The tired old green-and-white Chevy taxi groaned to a halt in front of a picturesque, single story, red brick house on Avenida Cinco de Mayo. Our driver, a middle-aged Hispanic woman, dressed in jeans and a Houston Oilers t-shirt with an unlit Lucky Strike dangling from her lips, neither asked directions nor initiated any conversation. She knew her job. When we arrived at our destination, she simply looked over her shoulder and gestured with her hand—we were there.

The neighborhood, what there was of it, was a barren desert area with a scattering of modest homes and shanties.

The front yard was surrounded by a white, waist-high block wall. A decorative wrought iron pedestrian gate serviced a walkway to the house, while a similar double-wide gate gave access to the driveway going to the rear of the house. Well-trimmed Bermuda grass accented by flowerbeds alongside the driveway and the sidewalk led to the front porch. Terracotta pots adorned the porch with a kaleidoscope of petunias, daisies, and a smattering of Wandering Jews.

I thought the place was beautiful, but incongruent with so much elegant color in the middle of...I was stuck, the middle of what?

The sound of the front door opening attracted my attention. A tall, muscle-bound gorilla wearing a wife-beater undershirt, jeans, and huaraches stood there like a welcoming committee to hell. His face was pock-marked and a scar ran the length of his left cheek. His nose was crumpled and flattened. He held a sawed-off shotgun in his right hand with the business end pointed to the ground. He bellowed out in Spanish, "Welcome. Come in. The boss will see you now."

I looked back over my shoulder at the departing taxi when we passed through the gate and approached the front step. The welcoming committee stood aside with a greeting, "We're glad you're here. The time is right."

Anna and I went into the living room, an art deco setting with a step back in time except for the wall-mounted flat screen TV. Otherwise, the décor was out of step with the surrounding barrio—a mauve Monaco-style sofa, two Trapezium turquoise shell chairs, an Indigo velvet ottoman, and an oval glass-topped coffee table in the center. Provence side tables rested alongside the sofa and chairs. The walls were tastefully decorated with Mexican and Mayan art—Folklorico and Flamenco dancers, a bullfight, a Frieda Gisele entitled *Woman in White*, and the almost-mandatory sketch of Pancho Villa.

Sergeant Sergio Mora entered from the opposite side of the living room. Not as large as the other man, he was solid and svelte, in his early thirties, wearing a white western shirt, khakis, and silver-tipped skull-and-crossbones toe-taps on his cowboy boots. His dark hair was cut to a flattop, closely shorn on the sides. He welcomed us with a broad smile, "Ricky, I'm glad you're here." He turned to Anna. "Madam, welcome to my home."

She extended her hand. "Agent Anna Fernandez, DEA."

"Thanks to both of you for being here. The time is ripe to castrate a couple of young bulls, if you know what I mean?" He gestured for us to be seated.

"A touch of Miami Beach," Anna commented when she sat in one of the shell chairs.

Sergio gave a soft laugh as he sat on the sofa. "You have a good eye, Agent Fernandez." He laughed again. "But I didn't have to go to Miami. Just Amazon." He glanced at the welcoming committee still standing in the doorway. "May I introduce one of our security agents, Pepe Salazar." He gestured to Pepe. "Drinks for our friends."

"Water for me," Anna said

"Same here," I replied.

Pepe propped his shotgun by the door and disappeared down the hall, returning moments later with a water pitcher and glasses. Sergio poured for each of us while Pepe took a seat on a bench near the door.

"Your Agent Soto in Juarez," he said while looking at Fernandez, "brought me up to speed on the Gonzales arrests and the situation with the ladies, including the little girl. If I may?" he asked. "I have a plan laid out and we can do it now, and I mean *right* now. There's no time to waste." He took a drink of water and continued, "I have no evidence at the moment to say this is Salinas family trafficking, but it's a high probability. The old man and his two young bucks pretty much have the run of northern Chihuahua—drugs, guns, sex. You name it and they do it."

I sipped my water, nodded agreement, and put my glass down on the coffee table. "That's the second time I've heard of the Salinas crowd."

Sergio chugged his remaining water, wiped his lips with the back of his hand, and dipped his chin in agreement. "They're bad asses, but what makes them so dangerous is they're too inexperienced. They jump without thinking and people end up getting hurt or dead."

"What are your thoughts?" Anna asked.

"We go now to Los Juguetes. An informant assures me the two women are still in the house, but things could change in an instant. Assuming it's the Salinas people, they could get pissed off and come and take it out on the ladies. We need to go now and pull them out."

Anna sat forward on the edge of her seat. "I've got a place we can put them up. The church in Mesilla will take them, and ICE has approved asylum."

The sergeant smiled. "Great place. I've been there a few times—some good priests, and the sisters are very kind ladies." A broad smile creased his lips when he looked at Anna. "You did good."

"Your plan?" I asked.

Mora gave a half-hearted chuckle. "Los Juguetes isn't a town or a village. It's an area at the end of the world—rocky, good-for-nothing mountains, rattlesnakes, some toy makers and a few farmers trying to feed their families. That's how your Gonzales family got wrapped up in this mess. They live on nothing and, if somebody is paying them good American money, they'll do almost anything for it. Plus, from my understanding of the Salinas family, the Gonzales men probably didn't have a say-so in the deal. Either do it or die right now."

I nodded in agreement. "I think I've got the picture. So now?"

"I can have a team together in thirty minutes." He looked at his watch. "It's three now. If we're loaded and on the road by three-thirty, we'll get there before five o'clock." He gave a sour expression and shook his head. "It's a disaster of a road—ruts, rocks tumbling down the hills, and maybe even some washouts. Expect it and, if somebody *has* graded it, then we're in for a pleasant surprise, but not likely. We should plan on it taking at least an hour to get up there.

"Once we get to the area, we go with a frontal assault. Full speed—get your goats and old ladies out of the way because we're coming through. The two women can bring a few things with them, and we're out of there. Five minutes tops. In and out. No messing around. There're too many loose cannons in the region. The good guys and the bad guys all look alike, so we don't take any chances. Bim-bam, thank you ma'am and we're gone."

"Tell us about the assault team," Anna said.

"We'll be in two SUVs plus a Toyota pickup. It has a .30 caliber machine gun, older than any of us, but it's a killing machine. Pepe stays here. Besides the three of us," he said with a swirling gesture between Anna, me, and himself, "we have three officers in one of the SUVs, two in the other, and a driver, gunner, and assistant gunner in the Toyota." He shrugged his shoulders and smirked. "It's not likely anybody will give us much trouble, but we won't hang around to find out."

"We're unarmed," Anna said.

Sergeant Mora tilted his head and smiled. "You won't be for long."

CHAPTER FIVE

Sergeant Mora took us in his Lexus SUV and drove to an industrial district on the southwestern edge of the city. *Fimbres Auto Reparación* was emblazoned over the double front doors. A teenager seated on a stool beneath an umbrella hopped up and pushed the sliding doors open when the Lexus rounded the corner.

Sergio slowed when we passed through the entryway and entered the darkened garage. Two lonesome fluorescent lights hung over the central drive separating a fleet of non-descript old cars, pickup trucks, a John Deere tractor, and an armada of black SUVs. He stopped midway the length of the garage when several uniformed officers emerged from an office near the back of the building. They were armed with enough weaponry for a war. One of them, a petite female, followed behind the others. She was dressed in military combat gear with a bullet-resistant vest, motorcycle helmet, and a sidearm slung on her belt. She walked toward a bright red Honda 250 dirt bike parked at the rear of the garage, mounted it with the ease of a veteran rider, and started it up.

Mora spoke softly, "Mandy Bustamante. She came to us from the Baja where she was a cross-country racer. We have to be careful with her. She's one sharp lady and has her act together, but she can get mad as hell at the cartel bastards. Her dad was a Tijuana cop and was beheaded, most likely by the Valencia family of the Tijuana Cartel." He gave a dour chuckle. "She's our point and she's good at it—can spot a bowlegged tarantula at two hundred yards, but I always have to remember that she has an agenda."

I commented, "Sounds like she's multi-talented, but point can be a suicide mission."

"Not for her. She's hell on wheels—can locate her target, get a fix, and report back before they have time to scratch their butts."

I shrugged my shoulders and nodded agreement. "I'm good with it if she is, but what should we expect between here to Los Juguetes?"

The sergeant's expression was somber. "We're in no-man's land once we leave town. At this precise moment," he expressed with a pointed finger at the spot in which we were sitting, "we're about two miles south of the border but in a different world. All *your* rules are off the table. Here, there aren't any rules. Whoever has the most toys in the end wins, plain and simple."

I didn't like it, but had to agree. I muttered more to myself than to anyone else. "Bastards. Kidnap a kid and sell her into prostitution."

"Yep," Mora said over his shoulder as he got out. "That's life when there aren't any rules. You just have to remember that the law and what's right are not necessarily the same."

Anna and I exited the vehicle and followed him toward their armed escorts who were climbing into two of the SUVs and the gun truck. The state police officers were all in their late twenties to mid-thirties. They wore military combat uniforms and bullet-resistant vests, had automatic pistols in their holsters, and carried AR-15 rifles.

Sergeant Mora snapped quick orders to them, then directed Anna and me into the two SUVs. Moments later, the caravan screeched out of the garage and onto the street with Mandy in the lead and the gun truck bringing up the rear. I rode in the back seat of the lead SUV. Jose was the driver with Sgt. Mora riding shotgun. Roberto sat in the back seat with me. I was now armed with a .40 caliber handgun provided by the Mexicans and wore a protective vest. Anna was in the second SUV, similarly attired and armed.

The caravan sped through a barrio of small businesses, each identified with homemade signs—*Tienda de Ropa*, *Farmacia*, *Abogado*, a scattering of *Licores* and *Restaurantes*, and what could best be described as low income government housing.

With horns bellowing and tires squealing, the motorcade cleared the way of youngsters playing kickball, mutts scavenging trashcans, and street vendors plying their wares. I held my breath as we drove with impunity through the narrow streets before pulling onto a major thoroughfare, the Guerrero/Lerdo Road, a six-lane boulevard without any traffic.

Minutes later, we were out of the city. The highway squeezed down into two lanes and coursed its way into the rocky, cactus-strewn foothills. A few miles further, it narrowed again and became a hardpan road crammed into a steep-walled canyon. Then, with no warning signs of the dangers ahead, the road nearly disappeared into a trail of ruts, rocks, and loose sand.

Mora commented, "We drive as fast as we can. They have eyes and ears everywhere, so they will have broadcast we're on the hunt. They don't know where we're going, but every bastard in the cartel is on guard." He shook his head in dismay. "The bastards. They don't screw around—shoot first and don't bother with questions." He exhaled with a hard blow and gave me a sidelong glance. "So we drive like hell and don't plan on taking it easy with anybody who gets in our way."

Our convoy bounced and swerved for the next forty minutes from one pothole to another, and from one drop-off to the next, but always ended right side up with all four wheels on the ground. I was thankful to be in the lead SUV. I had glanced several times over my shoulder at the trailing vehicles. They were buried in a cloud of dust—not a good day for allergies.

I couldn't help but feel déjà vu between today and Afghanistan. It was terrain like this when Bobby's vehicle hit the IED and was blown to pieces. It was a mid-afternoon, the sun glaring down, not an enemy in sight, in the company of trustworthy people, and *it* was over in an instant. My best friend and buddy from boot camp, our platoon's champion arm wrestler, was dead.

What about the cartel? I wondered. *They don't give a shit who they kill. They could do us right here.*

Our caravan crawled up the hill and leveled out on a plateau towering over the canyon we had passed through. We stopped to let the dust settle. Sergio looked over his shoulder at me and pointed to the road ahead. "We drop down another canyon and come out on the valley floor. We can't see Los Juguetes from here. It's around a bend to the right. We should be there in about twenty minutes, assuming no surprises."

Mandy sat astride her motorcycle alongside the lead SUV, the Honda engine grumbling. Like a tiger stalking its prey, she was ready to move on. Sergio nodded to Jose, who waved to Mandy. She didn't hesitate, hitting the power and pulling a wheelie to the drop-off at the lip of the plateau.

We moved forward precariously. After leaving the highland, we would be out of radio contact with any support personnel in Palomas. There was no room for error. We jostled between rocks and ruts for the next ten minutes, going from one hillside to the next. Mandy maintained a distance of about two hundred yards ahead of us, holding at a slow, cautious speed. If there was going to be danger, this is where it would happen.

We rode in silence, scanning the hills above and below the road. Afghanistan floated again through my mind.

The downhill ride was slightly better than the uphill we had traversed. Mandy increased her speed when the road began to flatten out, albeit still hugging the hillside. I watched her disappear around a curve only to see her reappear a minute later coming back toward us. She was hunched down over the handlebars, leaning forward and hard on the throttle.

Jose hit the brakes. The following SUV and gun truck similarly skidded to a stop, swinging as wide as possible on the mountain road, forming a firing line should we face an assault from the road ahead.

Mandy pulled alongside Sergio's window, removed her helmet, and wiped the sweat from her brow with her gloved hand. This was the first time I had seen her up close. She was beautiful—in her twenties, short brunette hair, bright blue eyes, pouty lips, but deadly serious.

"Roadblock, *Jefe*," she blurted in English. "They've dumped some rocks across our path. I stopped on a dime and caught movement out of the corner of my eye. It was two guys about one hundred yards farther down the road and about fifty yards up in some boulders. As soon as I saw them, they hopped on a couple of bikes, cranked them up, and were gone in a cloud of dust." She caught her breath, then continued. "They weren't expecting a point rider and didn't want anything to do with me. I'm sure one of them had a rifle or shotgun slung over his shoulder, but they didn't wait around for me to get a good look." She shook her head and continued, "Sorry, boss. It happened so fast I didn't get a good look at them, but they had bikes about like this," she said, patting her gas tank.

Following Sergio's commands, they juggled the vehicles until the gun truck could go around them. With Mandy in the lead, the column moved slowly down the road. A quarter of a mile later we came to the rudimentary roadblock—a dozen rocks, each about the size of a volleyball, but large enough to cause a vehicle to stop and become a sitting target.

Following their sergeant's directions, the two officers from the second SUV moved forward and up the hill. Minutes later, they waved back at us. They had found the bandits' hiding spot.

Mora glanced at me, "Let's surveil the area before we go any further."

"Gotcha," I replied as we got out.

We climbed up among the rocks and cactus and met the officers at the bandits' hiding place. I stepped back when Sergio moved ahead, extended his hand, and complimented the officers, "Good work. You might have saved somebody from getting killed."

"*Por Nada,*" each of them replied when they shook his hand.

He moved past them, got down on his hands and knees, and eased his way into their hiding place in the rocks. Speaking to no one in particular, he spoke in soft but commanding tones. "Excellent. You kept our crime scene sanitary." Scooting further into the crags in the rocks he held his hand out behind him, "Evidence envelopes, two of them."

Gael, the eldest of the two officers, immediately produced a business-size envelope from his trouser pocket, unfolded it, and put it in his supervisor's hand.

Out of curiosity, I stooped down and eased in by Sergio. I watched in silence as he used the tip of his pocketknife, lifted what appeared to be a marijuana joint from the dirt, and slipped it into the envelope. "The other," he commanded, extending an open hand behind his back.

Gael pressed the second envelope into his open palm with the smooth transition of a relay racer passing the baton.

I watched in silence as Mora reached out with his knife. He slipped the point into the open tab of an empty Budweiser can and carefully pulled it out of a little nook beneath a rock. He gave a gentle exhale as he put it in the envelope.

He laughed as he scooted back out of the hiding place. "DNA on an asshole or two," he said.

* * *

Ten minutes later we left the canyon behind and hit the open space of the valley floor. Los Juguetes was just ahead. It was little more than a scattering of aged, flat-roofed adobe buildings on a barren desert floor—no roads, no traffic, and no obvious signs of habitation.

Mora pointed to an abandoned church decimated by the ravages of time. Its bell tower stood forlornly over the empty shell, the windows long gone, and two front doors swung gently in the breeze. A mangy dog stretched out in the shade of the building lifted its head, barked once, then went back to its siesta.

"My informant told me they live about one-half mile up the hill behind the church," he said as he pointed up the gradual incline. "That's got to be it," he mumbled as we looked up at the whitewashed adobe structure, a tired sentinel on the highlands of Los Juguetes. Mora started to speak again when Mandy interrupted him, waving frantically at another equally squalid adobe structure down the incline to our left—the hand-painted word *Cantina* splashed above the door.

"Fijate, she yelled with her outstretched finger pointed toward two dirt bikes parked next to the door. "It's the same two bikes. I know it."

Mora grabbed his radio and commanded the second SUV and the gun truck to the *cantina*.

The day of reckoning was at hand.

CHAPTER SIX

J ose turned right and accelerated across the open desert to the
Gonzales home, skidding to a halt in a cloud of dust near the
doorway. There was no yard or sidewalk, just dirt and the adobe
house on the precipice of forfeiting its useful existence. For the
Gonzales family, though, it was home.

I took a moment to let my mind absorb what had happened
and, more important, what was *going* to happen. Nothing in the
Marines or DPS had taken me into the depths of the world in
which I was now immersed. Sergio had said it to me once before.
"There's not necessarily a link between what is right and what is
legal."

This wasn't a mid-East war we were fighting. We were no
more than forty miles from Hachita where my mother was doing
whatever mothers do in the afternoon. I took a deep breath. My
mind was set. We were going to get the women and go. It would be
the last day on earth for anyone who tried to stop us...or our last

day. One way or the other, the sun would set.

I followed Sergio to the front door. He bellowed in Spanish, "Police. You are safe." He repeated it when he banged on the double-hung door, the top open but the lower part closed. I stood alongside peering inside their squalid abode. A soiled couch sagged against the opposite wall, and the obligatory picture of Our Lady of Guadalupe hung on the wall to our left. A burning candle gave a soft glow from its place on a crate serving as an altar beneath the saintly picture, their spiritual hope in this life and the next. Otherwise, the room was austere, void of wall hangings or other furniture

A soft voice called out in Spanish from beyond the doorway to a room to our right. "Sir, we're coming. Give us a moment."

Seconds later, the women came into the main room. Abril was barefooted and wearing a faded short-sleeved blouse and tattered jeans. Her eyes were puffy and blackened. She offered a sickly smile, revealing her missing front teeth. Elise followed behind, grasping her daughter's hand. The elderly lady was hunched over, wearing a dirty cotton nightgown, and barefooted. Her hair was uncombed, and her face severely bruised and swollen. Like her daughter, her eyes were blackened.

Sergio's voice was respectful and soft. "Ladies, you are safe now." Making eye contact with each of them, he continued, "For only a short while, Abel, Emilio, and Felix are in custody, but all of you will be united and have asylum in the United States." He nodded and smiled. "You will be safe and have a good home and lives. I guarantee it." He twisted around and pointed to me. "He is an American police officer and he will take you across the border tonight, free to live as you choose."

I had to catch my breath when the women began to wail. They were overcome with joy but filled with anxiety about the road ahead as they hugged, cried, and looked about at their poor little home.

"We have almost nothing. Just each other," Elise said.

Sergio replied, "We must go now. Take what you need. There is no time to waste."

I stepped back when Abril went to the bedroom and returned with a bed sheet that she spread out on the floor. Within minutes, they had gathered a few clothes, some toiletries, and then stopped. Elise looked at Sergio and spoke, "One moment, please." Without waiting for a reply, the mother and daughter fell to their knees by the little altar, crossed themselves, and mumbled a prayer expressing their gratitude to the Virgin for her prayers and assistance. Then, without help, they stood, folded the four corners of the sheet to the center and tied a knot. Abril hoisted it to her shoulder while her mother retrieved the picture from the wall and pressed it to her breast.

She glanced at Sergio and smiled as best she could, "Ready, Officer. Thank you. We will go with you, of course." She paused and dabbed her eyes with her sleeve, then continued. "If we stay, those men may kill us. We know the way they work. They have done it to so many of our people." Then she asked hesitantly, "If we leave, what about little Catalina? What if they free her and she comes home only to find us gone? What will happen then?"

The sergeant lowered his eyes. His voice was soft, yet quaked with emotion. "They will never let her go, but we..." he said, gesturing back and forth between us, "we will never surrender. From this very moment, we will search for her." Shaking his head, he continued. "We will never give up...never."

* * *

By the time we were outside, Jose had opened up the third row of seats. He, Roberto, and Sergio helped the women climb in, then the officers handed their bundle and picture to them.

As I was getting in, Sergio ordered Jose to go to the *cantina* where the others had already taken control of whatever activity may have been occurring.

It took less than a minute for Jose to race across the desert floor and pull up to the bar. The Toyota gun truck and its two officers were standing by their gun, which was aimed at the bar door. Anna and the other officers were inside.

Leaving the women in the vehicle with Jose, Sgt. Mora and I got out and paused to listen. Hearing nothing, we went into the darkened confines of the *cantina*. I heard Anna talking, but it took a moment for my eyes to adjust to the darkness. It was a deadly serious scenario, but I almost had to laugh. Besides Mandy and the Mexican officers, there were only three other people in the bar. The bartender, a balding, rotund sixtyish man, sat on the floor beside a brass spittoon in front of the bar. Two young men sat on the floor amid the chairs and tables with their fingers interlocked over their heads. Each wore a western shirt, jeans, and cowboy boots. A double-barrel Browning 12 gauge over/under shotgun was broken open with two double-aught shells lying beside it on the bar.

Anna stood over the two young men, her hands on her hips, her face contorted in anger. Speaking in Spanish, she said, "Talk while you have a chance, or die trying to keep your mouth shut."

Mandy, who was standing slightly behind her, stepped around her American colleague and, without hesitation, pulled her Glock 9 mm from her holster and shoved it up the nose of the bandit closest to her.

The young man kept his fingers interlocked when he fell backward onto the floor with blood spurting down his face. He cried out in anger, "Fucking bitch, I'll kill you just like I did that little girl."

I knew immediately he had said the wrong thing.

In spite of Anna's attempt to hold Mandy back, the young Mexican officer broke loose and stomped on the man's face as he lay flat on the floor. There was a definite crunching sound as he fell unconscious, blood pouring from his nose and mouth.

Mandy stood in a rage, then stepped toward the other young man, screaming, "Next, asshole?"

"No. No. No," he barked. "You're crazy, lady. What the fuck do you want?"

She leaned in his face. "Catalina, you prick," she snapped as she swung with an open hand across his face. The slap echoed off the walls as the man rolled over on his side.

"Stop it, mother fucker," he screamed as he spit out a tooth.

Grabbing a handful of hair, Mandy jerked him upright on the floor and began her questioning of their basic data—full name, date of birth, address, education, and name of their employer. If they hesitated or stumbled trying to invent a response, she would not hesitate to bring them up to the present by either a swift kick to the balls or a slap across the face.

Divorcing myself from her process as much as I reasonably could, I walked behind the bar, found a bottle of *Anejo*, and drank it straight. Anna followed my lead. It was good for both of us.

Ten minutes later, everyone was loaded in the SUVs with the two bandits handcuffed, burlap bags over their heads, sitting in the middle row in front of Anna and her Mexican counterpart.

The two motorcycles were turned onto their sides and set afire with the unloaded shotgun laid across them.

The bartender stood at the door and gave us the finger when we pulled away.

CHAPTER SEVEN

The return trip to Palomas was long, bumpy, and delightful—wonderfully delightful. I didn't need another adventure.

Darkness was gathering by the time we drove into *Fimbres Auto Reparación*. The young man who opened the door for us hours earlier was still at his post, doing his job well. With Mandy in the lead, Jose pulled toward the rear office. He gave a strong exhale and exclaimed, "You're home, Boss. Another job well done." He turned and looked over his shoulder, speaking to the women, "Ladies, may we welcome you to your new life. Be assured, this man..." he said when he put his hand on Sgt. Mora's shoulder, "will bring your daughter home."

Mora gave a soft laugh and got out. I followed behind him while Jose and Roberto assisted the women as they clambered over the seats and put their feet on the dusty ground of the auto repair shop.

The second SUV and gun truck were only moments behind us.

When the vehicles were parked and occupants unloaded, Sergio spoke under his breath to Gael, then turned to Anna and me. "My supervisor, Lieutenant Espinosa, will call the Immigration desk and let them know we're coming. He'll also talk to your supervisor, Mr. O'Rourke. The Irishman should buy you a steak for what we did today, and nobody got hurt." He tossed a sidelong glance at me. "Well, almost nobody."

Anna tilted her head toward the handcuffed and hooded bandits who had been brusquely taken from the SUV and seated on the garage floor. "When do we interview them?"

"We'll put them in solitary—no food or drink should help us get their attention." Nodding approval of his own comments, he continued. "We have a secure facility a few miles south of town where they'll spend the night. Tomorrow they'll be served a couple of tortillas and a bottle of water." He looked directly at Anna. "I know you didn't approve of what you saw today and I didn't either, but here the rules are nebulous." He shook his head. "I'm not saying I like it, but it's a world much different from your side of Mr. Trump's wall. Here, every day is a fight for survival of the fittest."

"A cliché," Anna replied.

"Yes, and it's the rule we live by."

Anna shrugged. "What about the ladies?"

"We've got a small inventory of clothes in the back. I'll have Mandy get them presentable, then we'll take you and them to the border. Your people should be ready for them by that time. Then," he gestured with a sweep of his hands to Anna and me, "they're yours."

"What about our interrogation of the two assholes?" I asked.

"Same time tomorrow," Mora replied. "We'll be waiting for you."

52

* * *

It was nearly midnight by the time we cleared ICE. Abril and Elise would spend the next day or two in custodial protection while their papers were finalized, then we'd transfer them to Mesilla. In the meantime, we'd search for Catalina.

* * *

Some twelve hours later at our office, Anna and I completed the documentation of yesterday's activity and the path forward for the Gonzales family. We dined on Jimmy John's To-Go and crossed the border to Fernando's Hideaway. Following our quick beer and cab ride, we were sipping bottled mineral water in Sergio's art deco living room.

"I've talked to the custodians," Sgt. Mora said. "To borrow from that TV series, Bevis and Butthead had a quiet night chained to the wall in their solitary cells. Nobody had any communication or interaction with them. Our immediate goal was to neutralize them, to take away their bravado, and basically scare the shit out of them—make them feel alone and deserted. We transported them in separate vehicles so neither of them knew where the other was even though they were only about fifteen feet from one another." A smart-ass grin creased his lips. "They're learning what it's like to be powerless and think nobody gives a damn about them.

"The officers gave them something to eat and drink early this morning but, since then, they've been isolated without contact with anyone." He gave a sickening chuckle. "The protocol is to keep them confused and lost. That usually makes an interview go a lot smoother, but time will tell."

I scooted forward on the edge of the sofa, tablet in hand. "Okay, let's go over their personal data, then we can take them to the gates of Gehenna until we get Catalina back."

Sergio leaned back in the turquoise shell chair, pulled a note pad from his shirt pocket, and scanned Mandy's handwritten scrawl. "The taller guy is Oscar Davila. He's nineteen, and the one who had the shotgun. The other one, Butthead, is Ignacio Yanez. He's twenty years old and minus a few teeth and a broken nose, thanks to Mandy's little temper tantrum." The sergeant shrugged his shoulders and continued, "From what limited interaction we had with them, I think Oscar, or Beavis if you prefer, is the sharper of the two and he only lost one tooth.

"We didn't speak to them once we left here for our secure quarters. When we got there, no one spoke to them other than general directions of stand up and sit down," he said, nodding approval of his statement. "They haven't seen or spoken to each other since we took them into custody."

Mora plopped his water bottle on the coffee table, wiped his lips with the back of his hand and stood up. "Shall we?" he asked.

* * *

With Anna and me in the back seat, Sgt. Mora again rode shotgun with Jose at the wheel. Dissimilar to yesterday's trip to Los Juguetes, we went directly south on a paved road for thirty minutes, passing a few meager dryland farms before Jose slowed, then made a right turn onto a non-descript dirt trail. About two miles in, we came to what appeared to be a Mexican *hacienda* surrounded by a six-foot whitewashed wall with an arched gateway into the facility. A young man wearing a broad-brimmed hat, western shirt, jeans, and boots stood guard at the gate. An HK 416 rifle with a 60-round drum magazine hung on his shoulder—enough killing power for a small army. If needed as backup, an automatic pistol hung on his belt.

A cold chill ran down my spine. These people meant business and weren't to be screwed with. Sergio was right. It was a different world on this side of the border.

The compound lacked the touch of a family home. Nevertheless, it was a beautiful setting, reminding me of the Marquez ranch house near Animas. It was many years ago when Rosalinda and Victoria hosted a party and their father described it to me as 18th Century Spanish mission style architecture. It was whitewashed adobe with two massive hand-carved wooden doors, a red tile roof, and a wraparound porch. It was magnificent, clearly defining the headquarters of their sprawling ranch. They kept a meticulous Bermuda lawn surrounded by oleander bushes with potted plants on the porch protected from the blazing sun.

Here, the grounds were barren of landscaping or any decorative pots. It wasn't someone's home. It was hell on earth.

Jose parked at the foot of the steps leading to the porch where another guard stood, eyeing us through his mirror sunglasses. Like his counterpart, he carried the HK 416 with a drum magazine, plus a sidearm on his belt. He spoke Spanish to Sergio as we climbed the stairs. "Sergeant Mora, welcome back. Captain Flores is in his office." He opened the doors and stepped aside.

At first glance, I thought we had made a trip back to the "Giant" ranch headquarters in Texas. I almost expected James Dean or Rock Hudson to greet us. The furniture was massive wood and leather couches, chairs, and tables, all perfectly spaced throughout the main room, Paintings of what I could only guess were famous Mexican artists hung on the walls. The open-beam ceiling rose ten feet above the floor, and a full-mounted Texas Longhorn stood at the opposite end of the room. The setting screamed power, yet I knew its appearance belied the truth buried behind these walls.

A uniformed female officer stepped out from a side hallway. "Good afternoon, Sergeant," she said. "The captain is in his quarters but I've buzzed him that you're here. Please come in and have a seat." She turned and gestured for us to follow her. Midway down the hall, she guided us into the captain's office, an elegant and similarly furnished room with a window view over the pool in the rear patio. His enormous dark-stained wooden desk fit the overall décor as if designed for a Hollywood set, especially the *Reata*. The three of us took our seats in hand-carved wood and cowhide chairs. Moments later, Captain Flores made his entrance. A powerful looking portly but handsome man in his fifties, he exuded command presence. He was dressed in like fashion of his security officers— starched white western shirt, jeans, black cowboy boots with silver-tipped points, and a holstered pearl-handled pistol on his belt.

He introduced himself, offered cold drinks around, then sat down with his hands folded together atop his desk. He spoke with a professional demeanor. "Our guests had a peaceful sleep and enjoyed a light breakfast." He paused, then broke out in laughter. "The bastards were miserable, crying all night, and peeing their pants." He looked directly at Sergio. "I don't know what you told them, but they're scared shitless. I have no idea what you want from those worthless little *cabrónes*, but they'll tell you anything just to get out of here." He sat back in his chair, sipped his bottled water, and smiled when he glanced at each of us. "They're all yours. Just don't leave any dead bodies that require disposal."

CHAPTER EIGHT

I nga, the female officer we met earlier, and the three of us followed Captain Flores out the back door, then turned toward an outbuilding twenty yards to our right. From this distance, it could easily pass for a guesthouse or a shower and dressing area for the pool. It matched the architecture of what I already had dubbed the *Reata.*

My first observations were promptly dismissed when we approached the door. It was metal and locked from the outside by a padlock. Once again, a cold chill ran down my spine. I stepped toward the corner where I could see along the side of the building. There weren't any windows, nor did I hear or see any refrigeration or swamp box cooler.

Son of a bitch, I thought, *it's got to be 100 degrees out here and they're locked inside. I've lived in this desert. Beavis and Butthead are bastards, but this is crazy.*

I chuckled under my breath. *Whose side am I on?*

Inga took the keys from a keeper on her belt and gave them to the captain. He paused before inserting the key into the padlock, then spoke in English. "So we have an understanding, these men are not my responsibility. They're yours," he said, looking directly at Sgt. Mora. "They simply are my guests. I will feed, water, and house them, but nothing more. You take total responsibility for whatever transpires. *¿Entiende?*"

Sergio bowed his head slightly in deference to the captain. "Completely."

"You'll take them one at a time," Flores said. "The interrogation room is in the basement of the main building. They'll be handcuffed and hooded from their cell to the interrogation room. At that point, this is your cockfight."

Flores opened the door and stepped inside. Sergio, Inga, Anna, and I trailed in his footsteps. We were immediately hit by the stench and heat from the building's interior. The hallway was dark but for the daylight that shone in from the open door. I made out four sets of doorways opposite each other down the length of the hall.

Captain Flores tapped the dark wall with his fingertip. "Soundproofing acoustical panels," he said with a casual guffaw. "We like it quiet."

Sergio gave a thumbs-up and commented, "Let's start with Oscar."

The captain handed the keys to Inga, turned on his heel, and left.

She glanced at Sergio. "Follow my lead." She unlocked the second cell to the left and went in. I was only seconds behind her. It took a moment to adjust to the darkness, then I saw Oscar sitting on the floor next to a commode. His cell was approximately six feet wide and ten feet in depth. A five-foot chain was affixed to his left wrist and to the wall directly behind the commode. The walls and ceiling were acoustical tiles. The ceiling was punctuated with a dim light recessed in the center of the cell.

The young hoodlum didn't appear as tough as he did in the *cantina* when Anna and the others encountered him. Then, he was tilted back in a chair with his boots on the table, a smart-ass grin on his face, and toking a joint. Today he was barefooted, shirtless, and skinny. His face reflected unmitigated terror.

"We want to talk with you," Inga said.

Beavis looked like the proverbial deer in the headlights. He nodded his head but didn't speak.

Sergio grabbed the burlap bag from the floor and pulled it down over his head while Inga unhooked him from the chain, stood him upright, whipped his hands behind his back, and handcuffed him.

With Sergio guiding him by one arm and Inga the other, we went back the way we had come. Inga stopped unexpectedly when we were near the pool. She spoke in a commanding tone. "Take a deep breath."

Beavis did as directed, first one and then another.

"Do you smell the water?" she asked.

"Si, Señora."

"Good," she said. "Now remember this. We're going inside and down some stairs. We'll take the bag off once we are downstairs. I'll give you a drink, then you'll sit down and answer our questions." She leaned closer and spoke directly into his muffled ear. "If you play games with us, you will suffer severe consequences. Be truthful and get this over with. If you try to fuck us, we'll throw you in the water. It's about ten feet deep, has straight sides, and you are handcuffed. Most people cannot survive the first minute. Do you understand me?"

Oscar nodded. "Si, Señora."

* * *

The interrogation room was about 10' x 10' with a heavy wooden table in the center, its legs bolted down. A metal straight-backed chair faced the table and was also bolted down. A scattering of folding chairs leaned against the acoustical paneled walls. Light stanchions were in two opposing corners.

Sergio and Inga performed the activities she had described, then sat Oscar Davila in the chair. Anna, Sergio, and I sat across from him while Inga left the room. The sergeant reviewed Oscar's name and personnel data as a simple protocol to begin the questioning. The young man was hesitant, but then answered clearly.

Anna and I exchanged glances when we saw his heart pounding irregularly in his skinny body. His breathing was rapid and he appeared to be in a cold sweat. After a few moments, Anna spoke. "Are you sick?"

He strained to answer before choking out a nearly inaudible response in Spanish, "Dizzy. Pain. Arm."

Anna jumped out of her chair and took a key chain from her pocket. Sergio and I also recognized the situation and pulled Oscar upright while Anna un-handcuffed him. Urgency was written across her face. She looked at Sergio. "He's having a heart attack. Is there an AED?"

"I'll go look," he said, turning and darting up the stairs.

I turned toward Oscar as Anna eased him into the chair. He sat up for a second, made eye contact with her and smiled, then tilted his head and let out a shallow breath. Without uttering a word, Oscar Davila pitched forward on the floor.

He was dead.

* * *

Sgt. Mora had returned with the AED within minutes. Anna and I applied it as we had been instructed during our training but to no avail. We finally sat back on the floor and looked at Beavis' lifeless body between us.

Captain Flores, Officer Inga Perez, and Sergeant Sergio Mora stood motionless, looking down at the dead body. Flores glanced at Sgt. Mora. "You did no wrong. The stupid jackass put himself here. You had no way of knowing he had a bad heart. His treatment here was probably terrifying to him, but he was not mistreated." He shrugged his shoulders and continued, "The dumb shit may not have known he had a weak heart."

* * *

It wasn't relaxing, but Anna and I sat in the main room sipping ice-cold Modelo while we waited for the police ambulance. It wasn't a party mood, but we were high-centered and helpless. We had determined not to talk to Ignacio until his friend was taken away from the interrogation room. Plain and simple, we were in a holding pattern until the body was properly removed.

Ignacio had been given a light meal and water, but otherwise remained in his cell unaware of anything else.

The sun was cresting over the western horizon before the official police ambulance arrived—an aging Ford pickup truck, *Ambulancia* scrolled across the front of the hood, and *Policía* decals on the doors. It had a camper shell over the bed, and a single red light on the roof. The driver and attendant pulled around the side of the building to a gate where Inga met them.

We watched through the window in silence when they brought the gurney up from the interview room. The lifeless remains of Oscar Davila were in a black body bag and were loaded into the bed of the truck. We would never know what he had to say.

As foreign agents, we kept ourselves at a distance from what we professionally termed a "Custodial Death." This was a Mexican issue, not ours. We remained in the office while Sergio, Inga, and the mirrored sunglasses guard descended into the interview room carrying a mop, bucket, and a bottle of Clorox. It was a fact of life. Dead men always leave something behind.

It was seven o'clock by the time Ignacio Yanez was seated in the interview room. He would talk. The questions were simple and straightforward.

"Who do you work for?" I asked.

"Nicolas Salinas," he replied, appearing happy to perhaps see a way out by cooperating with the authorities. He continued without prompting. "I only met him once about a year ago. That's when I found out he owned the *cantina*. Me and Oscar were shooting pool and he was at a table with some men I didn't know. *Pelon*, the bartender, told us the boss wanted to talk to us. He nodded at Señor Salinas sitting there real cool-like, smoking a cigar and drinking tequila straight from the bottle." Ignacio cracked a smile with respect toward Salinas. "The guy was really cool. He offered us a good job and we took it."

The young Mexican shook his head and looked at the floor, then continued. His facial expression was so clear he had to be telling the truth. "If you lived like we did, you'd take the job, too. No questions asked. We didn't know what we'd do to earn it but, by damn, he paid us ten dollars right then. Faith money, he called it. He said he'd be in touch, but we never talked to him again, and that was a year ago."

Ignacio leaned back and looked up at the ceiling. "I'm not stupid. I knew we'd have to pull some shit, but what else could we do? Los Juguetes was a good village, but those days are over. All the toymakers have moved on." He paused and flicked the hair from his brow, then continued. "They do the same thing we do." He gave a self-deprecating grin and shook his head. "Man, you live like us, you don't have many choices."

"So when did the dope start?" Anna asked.

"Those people don't waste no time," he said. "The very next day the Salinas boys, Alberto and Federico, showed up. They were real assholes, being daddy's big shots and giving orders." He tossed a hard glance at Sgt. Mora. "They're the shitheads you should have here, not us."

"Fuck you," Mora fired back. "Their day's coming, but today is your day so don't screw it up."

"I want to talk about the two women and the little girl," Anna interjected.

Ignacio shook his head and looked down at his bare feet. "It was a fucking, pure and simple. The Gonzales men didn't show up at home the day after we gave them a load, so we knew there was going to be a mess to clean up. We just didn't know what it would be." He paused and looked at me, then to Anna. "Lady, I'm sorry about that. We didn't want to do anything to them."

Tears welled in his eyes as he wet his lips. "My little sister used to go to school with Catalina. She would come over and play at our house."

He stopped again and looked up at the ceiling as tears poured down his cheeks. "I'm sorry," he choked. "Those Salinas assholes came to my house before I was even up. They were real pissed and showed off like they thought they were big shots. Fucker Alberto jerked me out of bed, screaming at my mom to shut her mouth or he would shut it for her. Anyhow, he told me to get Oscar and to get Catalina, so we did. The bastard even told us to take care of her mother and grandmother. 'Do whatever you think they deserve,' he said. 'Kill the fucking cunts if you want to,' but we couldn't do that so we roughed them up a little bit."

"Where's Catalina now?" Anna asked.

"Right now? I don't know. I only know where we took her."

"Who is 'we'?"

"Me and Oscar. Did you already talk to him?"

Sergio exploded out of his chair, reached across the table, and grabbed Ignacio by the throat. "Don't you ask another question, you son of a bitch. We ask the questions and you answer them or I'll dump you into the pool and see how well you swim in handcuffs."

"Okay, man. Be cool. I didn't mean anything. So what do you want to know?"

"Catalina," Anna snapped.

Butthead Ignacio nodded his head. "She's gone. They told us to take *Pelon's* car; it's a Chevy Malibu. So that's what we did— whipped the shit out of the old ladies and took Catalina with us. Oscar went to the *cantina* and got the car. We stuffed Catalina in the trunk—tied up and gagged so she wouldn't give us any trouble. We took her to a house in Juarez."

"The address?" Anna asked.

"They wrote it down for us but I don't have it anymore. Maybe Oscar does."

"Can you show us the place?"

"Sure. But what do I get out of it?"

Sergio was faster this time, pulling Butthead Ignacio up by his hair and leading him to the stairway. "Little bastard, let's see how well you swim." He opened the door at the top of the stairs and shoved the kid outside with Anna and me following a step behind.

"Wait a minute, please," Ignacio pleaded as Sergio pushed him to the poolside. "Wait, damn it, I don't know how to swim."

I thought Sergio was bluffing, but he wasn't. With one hand on the back of his prisoner's head and the other in the small of his back, he gave him a hefty push into the pool. In no more than a second, he turned toward us grinning from ear to ear. "I'll get the prick out, but let him think he's drowning."

"Damn it, Sergio, this is going too far," I bellowed while Anna grabbed the pool broom and reached out for Ignacio. The terrified young man was underwater, his hands cuffed behind his back, kicking and struggling in ten feet of water.

"I've got him," Sergio said, taking the broom handle from Anna and slipping it under Ignacio's armpits.

The three of us took the broom handle in our hands and lifted the young prisoner's shoulders and head above the surface, then eased him into the shallow end where he put his feet on the bottom. He coughed and choked while he made his way to the steps, climbed up, then sat on the edge of the pool. Between spitting up water and bawling, he cried out, "I'll give you everything and everybody. I surrender."

Ten minutes later, a naked but dry Butthead sat at the interrogation table as a true believer. He was still handcuffed, and a towel covered his privates.

"I don't know the house number, but it's a really nice place in the Rincon Del Sol barrio, just off of Avenida de las Torres. They'll kill me and you, too, if they find us down there."

"We'll handle them," Sergio said. "Go on."

"It's a nice house. We pulled in the driveway and to the back of the house. They knew we were coming, and this tall, skinny guy came out to the car. All I know is what he goes by—*Matagente.*" Ignacio shook his head in disbelief. "Man, that guy scared the shit out of me. He's alive, but he's the husband of *La Señora de La Muerte.* I tell you, the son of a bitch is dead but he's alive like you and me. I know his reputation. In our business, things get around. The weirdo is a hired killer. I had heard of him, but now that I met him, I believe everything I ever heard."

"What did he tell you?" I asked.

"We got Catalina out of the trunk, untied the ropes, and took her in the house. Matagente told us where to go, so we went into an empty room. He told her to sit on the floor. She was scared out of her mind and sat down and cried—really hard.

"We left her in there and went in the kitchen and ate a pizza Matagente had, then chased it with a cold beer. We didn't know what to do, so we did whatever he said. He was real friendly, though, and told us we could spend the night—said he was principal, and this place was a school where girls learned to do tricks. He told us we could have one, but we said we had to get *Pelon's* car back.

"Officer, I'm telling you the truth. That is one bad dude. We ate the pizza and got the hell out."

"What about Catalina?" Anna asked.

"Matagente was going to teach her about her new job."

CHAPTER NINE

I was ready to strangle this measly son of a bitch, but bit my lip and went on about the business at hand. "The drugs," I said. "Before I lose my patience and wring your neck, tell us about your involvement in moving the drugs across the border."

My expression must have revealed the contempt I felt for him. He looked terrified and didn't want to try out again for the swim team.

"Nicolas Salinas is the honcho of the family, but he works for the Juarez Cartel. I know that because *Pelon* told us, and we believed him. There were too many strangers showing up around the *cantina*. They'd be there a while, Salinas would show up, then everybody would leave." He shook his head. "We'd have to be pretty dumb not to know there was some big shit taking place." He looked directly at Sgt. Mora. "I'm telling you, mister, you're getting into some heavy dudes if you think you're going to fuck with them."

"Worry about your own ass," Mora said. "I'll take care of us."

Ignacio shrugged his shoulders. "Okay by me, but you need to know Salinas runs the whole *Ascension* municipality. He lives on a ranch south of Los Juguetes, and *Pelon* said he's an underboss for the cartel—a heavyweight bad ass. Nobody screws with him. He doesn't touch anything dirty or give direct orders to anyone but his two boys, Alberto and Federico. They're the go-betweens. Everything comes down from Juarez to Salinas, then to his two boys, and from them down to people like us."

He paused, then continued. "Until this mess, we never had to do anything but move a little marijuana. Alberto and Federico would give the load to us. Normally, they paid us from three hundred to six hundred dollars, depending on the weight, to move it across the border. It was hard work, but it only took a few hours and we made some pretty good cash. Sometimes we didn't want to haul the load, so we paid some mules to do it for us and we'd split the money. That's how the Gonzales men got tied up in this. They had done it a few times before."

Butthead gave a casual smile and continued. "They never wanted to do it but, just like us, they needed the money."

I leaned forward and looked directly into his eyes. "So how did it go? Where did you cross the border? Who'd you deliver to?"

"The Salinas brothers showed us the first time, then we did it ourselves or showed the Gonzales men where to go. "We've got a place on a dirt road south of the border. It's a tunnel that starts on a hillside and goes down about seven or eight feet, then goes under the fence. We'd come out a couple hundred yards north of the fence and a few yards above an arroyo. The tunnel's about four hundred yards long. It was easy from there on. We would drop into the wash and stay in it until we got to the old train track.

"*Pelon* told us it was a perfect place because *La Migra* cameras or motion detectors couldn't see us, and he was right. It's kind of a long hike with a load, but we went under the highway to an old railroad track. There's a very specific old train crossing over the wash. It has a number fifteen painted on it. We would leave the load there. Somebody else would handle the payment," he said, shaking his head. "We never collected, but somehow the Salinas people handled the money.

"After we dropped the load, we'd bust our butts back down the wash, into the tunnel, and get the hell out of there," he finished.

I visualized it in my mind. I'd seen it hundreds of times—the old El Paso and South West Railroad line. It was more than a hundred years old—even the number fifteen. It was so clear I could see it when I drove up Hwy. 9 going back and forth between Hachita and Columbus. I would never have guessed it as a drop point for dope coming across the border. But apparently it was.

My mind was in a spin. There was so much to do.

Mirrored sunglasses, who we learned was Officer Geraldo Moreno, drove Anna and me back to the border in his spotless old Ford Bronco.

Sgt. Mora and Jose maintained custody of Butthead to begin his new career.

It was ten o'clock when Anna and I pulled into the parking lot of our headquarters. O'Rourke was standing in the doorway. A single overhead light tossed his lithesome shadow across the ground. He shook his head. "I don't know whether to congratulate or fire both of you." He extended his hand in a handshake and grinned. "I've been on the phone with Lt. Espinosa. He filled me in, *mas or menos,*" he cracked. "The coffeepot is on, so let's have a sit-down and you give it to me—all of it."

We talked and drank coffee into the morning hours, covering the generalities of what we had learned. Thus far we had not substantiated anything but tended to believe it was true, at least as far as Ignacio knew.

O'Rourke finally called it quits. We knew what we knew, and the rest would come later. I followed Anna and Miguel out, locked the office door behind me, climbed into my truck, and watched them leave. I was exhausted, mentally and physically. I was sitting in my pickup in our parking lot. The place was dark and deserted but for a scattering of lights around the perimeter fence. Everyone was gone except for the overnight crew staffing the camera and motion monitors.

It wasn't cold, but I was shivering. I couldn't remember the last time I had slept eight hours in my own bed, nor how many days it had been since I had spoken to Rosalinda, my Muncie.

My life had become entrenched in the world of the Gonzales and Salinas families and, of course, the dubious Beavis and Butthead, one dead and the other in more trouble than his young age would be able to withstand. I was caught up in an unending spiral of moral bankruptcy, narcissism, and greed, with life and death being swapped out like so many pieces on a checkerboard.

A couple of messages from Rosalinda showed up on my cellphone. Two days ago, she sent a simple little, "Hi," with a smiley-faced emoji and, at ten o'clock last night, another note, "Miss you. Tell me you're OK."

I responded. "Maybe 1 or 2 days before I can take time to breathe." I went through the gate and turned left toward home. No sooner had the gate closed behind me than my cellphone rang. It was her.

"Ricky, come to me," she said.

I gave a soft chuckle. "Rosalinda, I love you, but it's almost two o'clock and you have to go to work in a few hours."

She was crying. "I don't care. I can't live another day without you. Please, wherever you are, come to me."

My eyes watered as I pulled onto the shoulder and made a U-turn. She was my love, the woman I wanted to spend my life with. I missed her beyond description, and nothing could stop me from going to her. "Twenty minutes," I said. "Twenty minutes more; that's all I need."

"The door's unlocked and the candles are lit." She paused a moment, then continued. "I can't go another night without you."

Fifteen minutes later I approached her front door. Candlelight from her bedroom reflected through the windowpane. She met me at the door and stood there—the angel of my dreams. Wearing a black peignoir and barefooted, her voice floated like a spring breeze, "I love you, Ricky Basurto."

I took her in my arms and we kissed, then kissed again.

* * *

It was seven o'clock when she kissed me goodbye and I dragged myself into my trusty pickup and headed westbound on Hwy. 9 to Hachita, past the ignominious number fifteen on the trestle.

I slept three hours before Mom woke me up with a kiss on my forehead and a fresh cup of steaming coffee. "Ricky, you aren't getting enough sleep," she whispered as I propped myself up on the pillows. I managed a weak smile, stifled a yawn, and inhaled the delicious scent of real homemade coffee, not the sludge from the office coffeepot.

I was worn out, but happy. I had a mom who loved me, and a goddess from heaven who would spend her entire life with me. It couldn't get any better than this. All I had to do was resolve the human crisis with the Salinas and Gonzales families.

Nothing to it, just as soon as hell freezes over.

* * *

It was noon when I reached the office. O'Rourke was out to lunch, but I found Anna in the Data Analysis Office talking with Acacia Rios, the unit intelligence officer. Acacia's office was standard government blah, a 10' x 10' windowless workplace with a desk and PC workstation, a secretarial chair, and two straight back plastic chairs for visitors. A credenza behind the desk held an array of policy and procedure manuals, an overflowing plastic in-basket, an El Paso Intelligence Center (EPIC) manual, plus a series of manuals on the various Fusion Centers in the fifty states and the U.S. territories.

On the bright side, she had personalized her little haven within government regulations—a small framed photo of her pre-school-aged daughter holding a kitten on her lap, and a vase of peonies from her yard.

"Perfect timing, Ricky," Anna said when I walked in. She scooted a chair out for me and gestured for me to be seated. "We were just getting started with Matagente."

"Perfect," I replied. Anna and I sat back while Acacia went through the required data entry protocols, and followed it up with what little we knew about the man known as the Killer—Hispanic, about 55-60 years old, tall and thin, and terrifyingly ugly.

Acacia chuckled. "Hell of a description, but we'll see what comes up."

Moments later, her screen came to life. We sat stoically as the screen rolled over and over, then finally began to spit it out on the printer.

Acacia suddenly darkened the screen with a terse comment. "Secret data. Give me a moment to sort it out and I'll tell you what I can." At that, she rose and ushered us out.

We walked silently to the break room where I splurged for two cups of bland vending machine coffee, then made ourselves reasonably comfortable in the standard uncomfortable, low bid plastic chairs. Our conversation was forced bullshit: will we get a pay raise next year, is climate change for real, is the director going to retire?

We rambled about nothing while other agents retrieved their brown bags from the frig, the cleaning crew emptied the trash cans, and the HVAC tech thumped on the thermostat to cool down the building. No sooner were we resigned to being helplessly in limbo than Acacia stuck her head in. "Got it. Come on in."

We gathered in her office while she organized the sheets of documents the printer had spit out. "Sorry about the interruption, but it seems we have more than one malefactor with that handle. I had to sort them out and found the one you're interested in." She passed out a printed report to each of us. "I'll go over it, but I'm confident we have the right man."

I read the report as she recited the data.

Julian Espino Gatica

D.O.B. 11/6/58

74 inches tall, 155 lbs.

Place of Birth – Mexico City, Mexico

Occupation – No Legitimate Employment

Arrests – Numerous in Mexico: Murder, Assault, Rape.

Convictions – None

Suspect but not arrested in Mexico: Extortion,
Theft, Narcotics, and Sex Trafficking

Suspect but not arrested in Arizona:
Murder, Extortion, Weapons Violations, and Narcotics
No Other Data Readily Available
Mug Shot, Fingerprints, and DNA Profile
forthcoming in separate mail.
Signed – Agent Robert Dewey, El Paso Intelligence Center

"Okay," Acacia said, "but there may be something else of interest about this character, and it's upsetting. However, you must keep in mind that what I am about to tell you is unverified intelligence data."

I nodded and said, "Give it to us. What else could this shithead have been up to?"

"Maybe cop killing," she replied.

I threw a quick glance at Anna, then back to Acacia. My heart skipped a beat. "Not good. When, where, and to whom?"

"It was a Tucson PD undercover officer, Antonio Castaneda. He had worked up a major case on a legit Nogales import business that was also a major drug trafficking organization. To make a long story short, the case was about finished and he was leaving his office at the PD. He made it as far as the parking garage before he took a bullet to the head."

Antonio, I thought. *No, it couldn't be—not Mom's uncle. It's a small world, but not that small.* I forced myself back into the moment, the here and now. "Matagente?" I asked.

"He was a suspect, but it didn't pan out that way. Evidence pointed to a female accountant in the organization. There was nothing to directly say she and Tony—that's what he went by—

had an affair. However, attorneys for the import business as much as said so."

Goosebumps ran down my back. *Tony, that's what Mom called him.* I bit my lip. I had work to do. This was surreal, but it had to wait. I didn't have any choice.

Acacia shook her head. "Frankly, we don't know if there was an affair or not, but there was sufficient evidence to lead the Tucson PD and the Pima County attorney to believe Tony may have strayed. So, when the case was coming together, the bad guys put two and two together, killed him, and got rid of the primary witness in the case. There is a strong likelihood the woman did it. Her name *was* Mary Elizabeth Martin."

"Was?" I asked. "So what happened?"

Acacia gave a hint of a smile. "In a way, maybe justice was done. Mary and Reynaldo Guzman, her boss in the import business and the drug business, were both murdered in his hot tub."

"By whom?"

She shook her head. "No one was ever charged, but the intelligence says it probably was your man, Matagente."

"How did he end up in Juarez?" Anna asked. "Sonora and Arizona were Sinaloa Cartel territory."

Acacia shrugged her shoulders. "All I can say is basic intel indicated Matagente overplayed his welcome in Nogales and down the Baja. The Sinaloa bosses had a hard time keeping him under their thumb. He was pretty much an independent operator, so he found a new home with the Juarez Cartel." She chuckled as she continued. "Besides that, he's getting old. Being a killer is a hard life, so he found a place where he could do his thing, whatever that is, and not have to do all the work that goes with killing for a living."

Anna tilted her head and gave a sidelong glance. "He's a so-called school principal, and teaching kidnapped girls the sex slave business?"

Acacia returned the glance. "I think that's a pretty good description of your man."

CHAPTER TEN

Anna and I went in separate vehicles to Columbus for a late lunch where she introduced me to oriental food at Mama Chin's Café—shrimp fried rice, egg rolls, wonton soup, and green tea.

I had to admit; it was good.

We divided up the afternoon work over the last pot of tea. If the documentation was in order, she would pick up the Gonzales women from the detention center and deliver them to the convent in Mesilla. Then she would talk with the nuns or priests to encourage them to allow the teenage boy to stay there until more permanent arrangements could be made.

I would deal with Catalina and the Salinas family, but Uncle Tony would never be far from my train of thought. We walked out to the parking lot, nodded adios to each other, and went our separate ways.

Catalina was embedded in my mind. What was happening to

her at this precise moment? What horrors was she enduring? There wasn't a minute to waste. My lunch was good, but my stomach was rumbling. That little girl was depending on Sgt. Mora and me. I scolded myself. How could I take time for a meal while she was being tortured?

The answers were simple enough—it was introductory material taught by experts in our field. Take care of yourself. Have compassion for the victims, but don't become one yourself—a basic credo for undercover agents. Remember your personal being—your family, your profession, your moral code, and your mental health.

My mind was on fast-forward. First, we had to get Catalina, then we had to go deeper in the organization to make a case on the Salinas boys and their father. I would contact the Gonzaleses' lawyer, Adolph Mungia, bring him up to date on our work, and arrange a temporary release and interview with the adult Gonzales men. There was a lot to do—all of it high risk.

I called Mora and set in motion a meeting within the hour. Instead of me crossing the border, he would leave his vehicle and walk across. We would meet in the parking lot of the Duty-Free Extravaganza Shopping Center a couple blocks north of the border crossing.

I went to the Dairy Queen for a vanilla cone to settle my now-bubbling stomach, then parked in the parking lot of the Extravaganza.

Mora was on time. He climbed in, took one look at my ice cream, and said he wanted one, too. Ten minutes later, we were back in my truck, talking business. Listening to him, I was impressed by how organized and detailed he was. The Chihuahua State police officers were not corrupt or slapstick jokers. While they lacked the technical expertise and hardware we had, they were highly skilled, professional cops.

He had taken fingerprints, blood, and hair samples from Oscar and Ignacio, and provided me with a sample of each. He had not run records checks on any of the Salinas family for concern the system was tainted and would give the Salinas group and the Juarez Cartel insight into our operations.

However, one of his confidential informants provided him some background on *Pelon*, the bartender. *Pelon* was an American citizen, born and raised in Seminole, Texas. His true name was Sixto Fajardo. There may have been an old warrant, possibly quashed because of its age, for felony assault, burglary, and evading arrest. *Pelon*'s parents had lived in northern Chihuahua, but met their fate during the drug wars as the cartels battled for territory. It was alleged his parents had lived in Mexico off and on over the years, serving as a conduit for drug traffickers. When they lived in Texas, they continued their trafficking activity and that was when their conflict with the cartels boiled over. They were summoned to a meeting in Juarez and were never seen again.

"The little girl?" I asked. "Where are you on her case?"

"It's touch and go. I assigned four of my officers to the detail last night. They went in two vehicles and had young Yanez in one of them. He was pretty accurate with his directions and, by two o'clock this morning, they had identified the correct location. It was exactly as the kid described—a pretty decent barrio, clean, no shootings going on, no drunks or addicts sleeping in the gutter. The house was a large single-story adobe structure. It had a low patio wall around the front yard, then it wrapped around to the back and sides, about six feet high.

"We called in one of our technical crews this morning," he continued. "They were disguised as utility workers and put surveillance cameras on a pole on the street and another covering the back alley. Later this morning, Gael and Mandy rented an apartment in the next block to the west of our target. They're able to monitor the cameras from there, plus they record the videos if we need them later.

"I talked to them before I got here. They said there hasn't been any traffic to the house other than a delivery from the Mennonite Cheese Store." Mora paused and cast a glance at me. "Hey, *amigo*, Mennonites are big in cheese here."

"Well, you got me there," I said, "but this isn't the time for me to learn about the Mennonites. So, what did you make of it?"

"Nothing," he said. "We know nothing now, but we will. This is Thursday. Let's see what happens tonight or over the weekend."

My brain tweaked—Thursday. A lot of bad things have happened in the Thursdays of my life. I shivered, then got over it. This was real life.

"What about Catalina or any others that might be in there?"

Mora licked the last of the ice cream, then stuffed the remnants of the cone into his mouth. "I know you want to get in there. So do I, but we need to be sure what's going on and who is there before we charge in and clean house."

I was disappointed, but understood. We would only get one chance and had to make sure the time was right for us to do it—too early or too late, and we would blow it forever. We bade each other goodbye, and Mora hopped out and started toward the border crossing. He was nearly out of the parking lot when I saw him stop and put his cellphone to his ear. He froze momentarily, then turned and ran back toward me. He pulled the door open and jumped in, grinning like a kid with a new skateboard.

"They just saw that skinny prick go out to the street and meet a woman. They talked for a few seconds, then she left on foot, and no, we don't have any idea who she was. We didn't have enough people to put a tail on her, so they had to let her go. They don't know where she went, but she came back a few minutes later with our little girl. The bitch was holding Catalina's hand and went to the front door. Our people couldn't see who let them in, but the female sent Catalina in, looked back over her shoulder, then went in and closed the door behind her."

"So Catalina and Matagente are both there right now?"

Mora nodded. "*Seguro*, but we don't have any idea who, if anyone else, is also there."

"We gotta go," I said.

"10-4. Come on. Let's do it."

* * *

Two hours later, Mora, Mandy, Gael and I, along with three more of his officers, gathered in the Juarez apartment. No one was in uniform. We could see the front of the house, plus we had a camera focused on the rear. Nobody had come or gone. Catalina should still be there along with the woman, Matagente, and who-ever else we didn't know.

The plan was straightforward. There was no evidence of a re-inforced door, so the three officers would go to the back and the four of us to the front. We would each wear a tactical vest with clear lettering, *Policia*, on the front and back. We would knock and announce, then enter with shock and awe. Each of Mora's officers carried an AR-15, a sidearm, and one man at the front and another at the rear had a doorknocker—a steel twenty-pound battering ram.

It was exactly five o'clock when we left the apartment for the short jog to the house. We gave the rear entry crew thirty seconds, then hit the front door. It folded like a piece of wet cardboard. Mora and Gael led the charge in the front with Mandy and I on their heels. Mora was shouting at the top of his voice, "*Policia!*"

The officers in the rear were doing the same.

Matagente bolted out of a side room with a handgun at the ready position. All of us were screaming, "Policia" but, as the cop saying goes, "It was over before it started." A dozen or more gunshots rang out and the skinny, ugly gunman was flung back against the wall, froze for what seemed like forever, then slid to the floor in a pool of blood. The pistol was still in his hand when Matagente joined the fabled personification of death, *La Señora de la Muerte.* Any chance of talking to him about Uncle Tony died with him.

I heard two distinct female voices screaming in terror from a back room. Mandy and I hurdled Matagente's body, raced down the hall, and threw open a bedroom door. Catalina's naked body was tied spread-eagle on a bronze bed frame. The woman we had seen in the video was also naked. She cowered on the floor beside the bed. Terror scrawled across her face as she pleaded, "*Perdóname. Él me hizo hacerlo.* He made me do it."

I pulled a pocketknife from my pocket and cut the cords binding the young girl to the bed while Gael grabbed a blanket from the floor and covered her. Mandy, as she was inclined to do, swung a haymaker across the side of the woman's head, knocking her backward into a state of unconsciousness.

Seconds later, the scream of sirens of Juarez's finest roared down the street. Sgt. Mora ran out the front door, holding his badge over his head and shouting, "*Policia Estatal!*"

The older woman was struggling to sit up when Gael grabbed her hair and pulled her into the hallway.

I remained with Catalina while Mandy searched the chest of

drawers, found her clothes, then invited me out while she helped the child get dressed. I looked back just once. Catalina's entire body was shaking. Tears poured from her eyes. She was so unsteady that Mandy had to hold her upright. I couldn't guess what had happened to her and really didn't want to know.

I stepped over Matagente's body but slipped in a gathering pool of his disease-infected blood. I caught myself against the wall and looked down at my boots—the crimson red ooze was splattered all over them.

I took a deep breath, ignored the mess, and went outside with Sergio. He and a municipal police lieutenant were huddled on the sidewalk. A dozen or more uniformed municipal officers deployed round the perimeter, blocking off the curious neighbors and the ever-present TV photographers. I joined them briefly, then took my leave and returned to the rented apartment and out of view of the myriad of photographers swarming the barrio from every direction.

Once inside, I found the well-stocked refrigerator with an assortment of beverages. I chose one of the stronger of their selection, *Noche Buena*, a Mexican/German lager—a brew I couldn't find in New Mexico. Once I had satiated my thirst, I sent a text to Miguel, Anna, and Mungia—we had recovered Catalina. I smiled inwardly. *Salinas, here we come.*

CHAPTER ELEVEN

I t was ten o'clock when I reached our desert headquarters to meet with Acacia, Anna, and Miguel. I chuckled under my breath. The old adage was still true—it was over before it started. That's how fast things happen in our business—hours or days of boredom, then a few seconds of hell on earth.

We gathered in Miguel's office to review the day's activity with my colleagues. It didn't take long to assess the entire scenario since the actual goings-on were in the Mexican's domain, so I had been little more than an interested onlooker and hadn't discharged my weapon.

We had been sitting there a few minutes when I looked down at my boots. Matagente's blood was going to be hard to get off. Maybe I would just throw them away. I'd get some new ones like Muncie's—a pair of Old Gringos, an excellent boot maker.

Our primary goal of rescuing Catalina Gonzales was achieved, but she had paid a heavy price for being a child victim of the drug wars. The medical personnel of *Cruz Roja Mexicana,* while working in the environment in which they were sometimes victims of *La Linea* bombings, proved to be exceptional in the care they gave to her. Furthermore, *Casa Amiga*, the rape crisis organization, provided outstanding love and attention to their young charge.

Mandy stayed with Catalina until she was treated at the hospital, then transferred to a Casa Amiga facility until she could be reunited with her family.

Sergio had provided me with photos of the crime scene—the exterior of the house, multiple views of the interior, a variety of shots of Julian Espino Gatica's last foray, a set of his fingerprints rolled from his lifeless hands, and samples of his blood and hair for DNA purposes.

The good sergeant also provided me with the photos, fingerprints, and blood and hair samples from the adult woman—Olivia Beltran. She was fifty one years old, and Matagente's common-law wife. She and the killer/sex trafficker had been together in the Baja and had come to Juarez several years ago. She admitted under Mandy's questioning to being involved in the various sexual activities their "students" would have to master to earn their keep.

Julian Espino Gatica would be one of the few identified bodies to go to the *Cuidad Juarez* Morgue today, not like the dozens of other drug war victims lining the cold storage chambers.

It was eleven o'clock before we called it done, at least for tonight. I signed all of the evidence sheets, put the tagged property into the secure lockers, and went home. I would have a whole night's sleep in my own bed.

At least I could *hope* for a good night's sleep. Uncle Tony would have to wait. I couldn't talk to Mom about him. It would make her worry even more than she already did. No, I would do it my way.

* * *

Anna was in Mesilla dealing with the two women and helping them make arrangements to move Catalina across the border, no small ordeal in these times of a growing immigration problem.

I was torn by where to start—the Gonzales men and the dope trafficking, or Uncle Tony. Who would come first?

When I pulled into our secure lot, by chance, Acacia was parking nose to nose with me in her personal car, a new Kia. Seeing her made me believe it had to be a premonition: Tony first.

"Got a few minutes?" I asked when we approached our office door.

She smiled. "You had a heck of a day yesterday." She gestured with her head, "Come on; what can I do for you?"

Twenty minutes later, she sat back with her hands clasped beneath her chin. "Ricky, I've never heard of such a story. Of course, I'll help you out, but let's keep this to ourselves for the time being. We don't need nosy people who want to help." She gestured with her finger back and forth between the two of us. "We'll pin this down and, assuming it comes out as it appears, then we... or maybe I should say *you* and your family can decide what, if anything, you want to do with it."

I nodded and gave a soft and very sincere, "Thank you."

"About fifteen years ago?"

"I think so, but I never pushed my mother about any of the details."

"And don't," Acacia replied. "I've got resources enough to get what we need. After that, you and I will review it, then the ball is in your hands."

"Any idea how long?"

She chuckled, "Ricky, that's what all you cops ask." She gave me a polite smile and continued. "If I need anything, I'll let you know. Otherwise, trust me. I'll get it done."

* * *

Anna and I texted each other back and forth. She was going to be busy today and maybe tomorrow with Catalina and the two women, so I would get busy with Abel and Emilio. We each had important tasks facing us, so we needed to work quickly but carefully. There was no room for errors.

I met Mungia in the reception area of the El Paso Detention Center and we reviewed my plans for working with his clients for my criminal investigation and for their future. Afterward, I met with the shift supervisor and signed the Gonzales men out for a Temporary Investigative Interview.

Twenty minutes later, they walked out of the locked doors, free men, at least for now. They wore the same clothing they had when we arrested them in Julian Wash—jeans, work shirts, straw hats, and boots. There was one exception now; each of them wore a smile. They smelled fresh air.

"Let's take a ride and talk," I said when we got to my truck. They got in with Abel in the middle and Emilio riding shotgun. We zipped up on I-10 westbound. Speaking in Spanish, I began our conversation with a soft opener. "Hungry? I'll get us some lunch."

Abel chuckled. "Real food?"

* * *

The lunch rush was over when I slipped into a parking spot at *Molina's Restaurante* on Hwy. 11 south of Deming. We took a booth in the rear corner, away from the scattering of customers. Our conversation thus far had been a general discussion about Catalina, the men's wives, Felix, and their sought-after redemption of life in the United States. Once we were seated and had given our orders, my first thought was to test them. How open and honest would they be, or would they choose to give me just enough to get by, but no more?

"Tell me how you got into bringing dope into New Mexico."

They glanced at each other, then Emilio spoke on their behalf. "You're an honest officer, Mister Basurto. We trust you, and we want you to trust us." He looked at his dad, then back to me. "We're not drug traffickers. We're workers. Toymakers, plus any odd jobs we can get to put food on our tables." Shaking his head, he continued. "When the cartel speaks, we listen. Everyone does. They have guns and money, kill for sport, and torture because it's fun to watch people die. We're not like that. All we ever wanted to do was to work, serve God, take care of our families, and someday die and go to Heaven. That's who we are."

I leaned forward on my elbows, speaking forcefully yet politely, "I understand and hold no ill will toward you, but tell me about how you brought drugs into New Mexico."

Abel gave a self-deprecating chuckle. "It was too simple, at least until we got caught. I have to believe someone tipped you off because the route had been safe for many months."

I nodded and smiled. Of course, he was right. "Go ahead; tell me," I said.

"It was those two boys, Ignacio and Oscar. We know they worked for the Salinas boys and *they* worked for their father." He looked down at his feet and shook his head in disgust. "People like us don't have a chance. Do it or die. It's that simple, so we did it. I have to admit; we needed the money or we'd starve. They paid us two or three hundred dollars every trip we made. That's more money than both of us together would earn in a month, so we did it."

"Details," I said.

Emilio spoke first. "You want details? Okay, I'll give them to you." He paused when the waiter delivered our food—tacos, frijoles, and lettuce and tomato on the side. Each of us had iced tea.

We took a few minutes to begin our meal before Emilio continued. "We carried it across six times before you caught us. Always marijuana. On the last two trips, we took Felix along to help haul it since one of us would carry a shotgun." He shook his head and grimaced. "Things were getting dangerous—too many people from Central America, too many coyotes, too many guns. It was getting scary."

He paused to sip his tea, but I prodded him on. "Don't stop. I want to know everything."

"Sure," he said, "and we'll give you everything. We had nothing to lose. Tell them 'no' and they'd kill us. So we did it."

"There's more," Abel said. "The tunnel. You know about it, don't you?"

"You tell me," I replied

"Those two young boys showed it to us the first time, and we used it every time until you caught us."

I nodded affirmatively. "Go on."

"We drove to about a quarter-mile from it in *Pelon*'s car. The entrance is well concealed in the creosote bushes, so we just dropped down into it. We each had a flashlight, and we'd leave them there for when we got back. We would carry the marijuana through the tunnel and come out on your side of the fence by a dry wash. We'd follow it until we got to the drop point at the old railroad crossing over the arroyo. We'd dump it there and leave. Someone else would take care of it and the money—end of story. We'd get paid after we got home."

I sat back and sipped the tea. It was good.

"Mister Basurto, if I may, sir, there is more if you please," Abel said.

"*Seguro*," I replied as I sucked on my ice cubes.

"When I was young, maybe thirteen years old," he began, "my father, God rest his soul, worked during the summer in the Colorado and New Mexico mountains. In those days it was legal. He had a green card. He worked for a private service provider who had contracts with the Forest Service. It was hard work but paid well. I helped out and they paid me a dollar every day. Really, I didn't care about the money. I was with my father and we were earning money for food and school. It was a good life, and I learned a lot—especially about the aspen groves." He paused and cracked a hint of a smile. "And here is where *you* can learn something, Mister Basurto. The aspens are a lesson in real life. They are like the cartels. They have roots and sprouts. You can't kill them."

"I don't understand," I said.

"Some gringos may think of me as a dumb Mexican, but I know how the world spins. I know honesty and corruption, the difference between hard work and stealing, the good and the bad in people of all walks of life." He looked down at his plate, then raised his eyes to mine. "You're a good and honorable man, but you're fighting a losing battle. This one is going to the bad guys because people have changed."

He leaned back and smiled more to himself than to me. "My people used to hand carve good quality children's toys—little cars and trucks, wooden painted dolls. Children loved them. They played day and night with our toys, but the times changed. They don't even play with one another anymore. They simply sit on their butts and play with their electronic toys. They want a world outside of Los Juguetes.

"The young people, not just where we live, but everywhere, want a world much different than ours. And that brings me to my point on why you're fighting a losing cause—the aspens, remember?" he asked.

"Sure, but I'm not following you."

Abel leaned forward and ate the last of his frijoles, then continued. "Aspens grow in groves. They're deciduous trees and can live 150-200 years, but that's not the whole story. The real story is their root system. That's why you find them in groves and not just one here or there. Aspens are a connected family through their roots. Sure, they have seeds that are blown by the wind, and some of them take root and grow." He chuckled and continued his story, smiling, clearly enjoying telling his parable. "You can chop a tree down, you can burn it to the ground, but the secret is in the roots. They spread and grow sprouts, and sprouts become trees, and life continues. And that, my friend, is why the cartel is like an aspen grove.

He leaned back in his chair, lunch finished. "You can kill the bastards. You can throw them in jail, do anything you want with them, but their root system is alive and well. Their seeds are spread as though by the wind. Their way of life continues because people want what they have: money, power, and all the things that money can buy.

"The aspen grove is beautiful, but its life depends on its root system. The cartel is not beautiful," he said. "Their real source of life is underground. Pick one off, and another pops up to take his place." He shook his head and gave me a sidelong glance. "But you will never get rid of them. Our way of life is over, and maybe yours is, too."

* * *

We left *Molina's*, drove south to Columbus, then west on Route 9 before I swung south on a caliche trail alongside Julian Wash. I pulled up on the little mound beneath the lone mesquite tree, the same tree Chuey and I had parked under that day.

Abel gave a half-hearted laugh. "Now I see how you found us. We had just gotten out of the tunnel and were getting into that wash. One more minute and we would've been out of sight of you and your cameras."

"Yep," I replied as I opened the door. "Let's go down and you can show me the entrance to the tunnel."

We stepped it off—roughly five hundred twenty-five yards from the truck to the tunnel. "Son of a bitch," I exclaimed as I stood over the hole in the ground. It was centered in the middle of a small patch of mesquite trees and creosote bushes, no more than two feet in diameter. The entrance was covered with a single sheet of plywood. The entryway sloped down five or six feet into the tunnel. The flashlights they had carried lay in the dirt nearby.

Abel looked forlornly into his personal pit to hell. "It was a terrible day," he said when he looked up at me. "Not for Emilio and me, but for my wife and daughter, and even worse for little Catalina." Tears poured from his eyes. He choked, then leaned over and vomited. Going to his knees and spitting, he uttered a mournful prayer, "God in Heaven, forgive us our trespasses... Please cleanse that innocent child of this terrible deed. Make her whole again."

Emilio knelt beside him. They hugged and wailed, their cries reaching out over the barren desert. I turned my back, but their cries stung my soul.

For a moment, the desert creatures—the coyotes and rabbits, the snakes and lizards, even the trees and cactus—all stopped in reverence to the prayers that were raised from this lonely place.

* * *

We returned back up the dirt road to Hwy. 9, where I turned left for a quarter-mile to the point it passed over Julian Wash. Abel looked to the north, the infamous rail crossing with the number fifteen emblazoned on the trestle a mere two hundred yards from the highway.

He grimaced. "I wish you could blow it up."

* * *

We stopped at Dairy Queen where each of us had a chocolate shake, then turned back up the highway to El Paso. There was no further need to continue with any questions. I knew what I knew. There was nothing else. We had stopped fifty kilos of marijuana from being distributed on the U.S. market, and a hard-working, honest family had been destroyed. Of course, I couldn't forget Oscar. He was dead, Ignacio was going to prison, and the Salinas family had yet to be dealt with.

That was the price of our little war.

CHAPTER TWELVE

I left them at the El Paso Detention Center with the promise I would notify Mungia in the morning with the approval to complete their asylum request. They could join their family. In my mind, though, I knew they had a long and strenuous pathway ahead. It would not be a bed of roses, but more like the road to perdition.

I called Rosalinda when I got in my pickup. She grabbed it on the first ring. "Ricky, where are you? Can we have dinner tonight?"

I swung westbound on I-10 with a smile on my face, the first one in a long time. "I'm just leaving El Paso. Are you home?"

She chuckled. "*Ese,* I work, too. No. I'm not home. I'm hot and dirty; how's that for a description of your fiancé?"

"Even dirty people have to eat," I said. "I can pick you up in an hour."

"Ricky, I left the Wilderness Study Area about twenty minutes ago. There's a major dig going there, but I can be home in a little bit. Why don't we eat at my house—just the two of us, and not talk about work."

"You're music to my ears. I'll be there."

We did it. Scrambled eggs and chorizo, tortillas, Negro Modelo, and the conversation was what it should have been—when and where to be married, where we would live, how many children? There was much to talk about, and it felt good. It was a semblance of real life, and we were real people.

I was home and in my own bed before midnight. It had been a perfect and long overdue evening. I didn't think or dream about work. It was the best night's sleep I could remember...until the phone rang. I rolled over without opening my eyes, groping for my cellphone on the nightstand. I didn't look at the caller ID.

Her voice scared me. "Ricky, have you seen the news?"

My heart jumped. Rosalinda. I grabbed the clock—it was 6:10. The sun was barely squinting through the drapes. "No," I barked. "So why are you calling me at such a weird hour?"

"Ricky," her voice wasn't angry, but strong and compelling. "You were on the news. I saw you on the Good Morning Show from Juarez. They had everything about that case and they showed you and your Mexican *compadres* out on the sidewalk. You were gathered together and talking. They had a close-up of your profile, and said your name."

"What?" I blasted.

"Yes, Agent Enrique Basurto of the New Mexico State Police and a member of an elite task force intercepting sex traffickers and drug dealers."

"They said that?"

"Yes, Ricky. They gave your name and who you work for. They shouldn't have done that, should they?"

"Fuck," I growled. I was wide awake now. "Thanks, Muncie. I'll be talking to you." I didn't wait for a response before I shut down my phone. This wasn't an ideal way to start a day.

* * *

I arrived in the office ahead of the others and assumed I'd have an early start heading off the proverbial pile that would come downhill. I was wrong and I was pissed. I had left my cellphone at home.

Miguel O'Rourke, my supervisor and the man who controlled my career had left a handwritten note on my desk:

1. Be in the Las Cruces Supervisor's Office at 9 sharp.

2. Find your cellphone

M. O.

I didn't waste time as I ripped a fast trip home, said "hi" and "bye" to Mom, and was in the Border Patrol office in Las Cruces ten minutes early. O'Rourke was seated in the anteroom, outside the secure area behind the bullet-resistant windows and locked steel door—a sign of the times.

He tossed aside the worn Time magazine he had been reading, stood, and extended a hand in friendship. "Shit rolls downhill," he said, "but I think we can head this off." He gave me a sidelong glance, shrugged his shoulders, and turned to the control officer in the booth behind the window. "*Listo*," he said with a wave to the officer.

We passed through the security access and down the hall. Miguel led the way and opened the door into the conference room. The inner sanctum consisted of a mahogany conference table surrounded by a dozen straight-backed chairs, not the cheap plastic ones like we have in our meeting room.

The Border Patrol sector chief sat at the far end with their civilian public information officer to his right, and my Highway Patrol lieutenant, Oscar Soto, to his left. The New Mexico flag was in the corner behind the chief, and the American flag was in the opposite corner.

My first thought was, *Hmm, very official. I wonder when was the last time they were on the scene when somebody was killed.*

Soto gave a half-hearted smile and a similarly voiced, "Have a seat."

I pulled out the chair at the end opposite the chief and sat down. Making quick eye contact with the men I considered my inquisitors, I voiced my own, "Good morning, gentlemen." Meanwhile, O'Rourke pulled up a chair in the corner near the door behind me.

"Officer Basurto," the chief said, "exactly how did you happen to have a starring role on Juarez TV this morning?" He didn't wait for a response before he continued. "Of course, it's very newsworthy in these immigration-challenging times, so it's been picked up by the networks." He looked straight into my eyes. "Damn it to hell, Basurto, did you know the president of the United States saw you in his morning intelligence briefing?"

I started to speak, but he cut me off. "I'll tell you when I want you to speak, but right now you need to sit there and listen. By shit, I'd like to fire you. You had no damned business down there raiding a whorehouse and killing that jackass pimp. Do you hear me?"

I started to speak again when Soto raised his hand to stop me. "Officer Basurto, we've reviewed Agent O'Rourke's report, so let me make sure I have this correct."

I nodded as he spoke. "You and Sergeant Mora of the

Chihuahua State Police investigated a drug and human trafficking case in which you and Agent Chuey Molina apprehended two adults and a juvenile who were armed and importing marijuana. Is that correct?"

"It is, sir."

He continued. "After the arrests, was a little girl kidnapped by cartel members, and her mother and grandmother severely beaten?"

"That's right, sir."

"Is it true you and Agent Anna Fernandez arranged to provide asylum for them and to the men involved in this case in exchange for them assisting in prosecuting cartel members?"

I nodded. "Yes, sir."

"Has the young girl been rescued from that house in Juarez where she was undergoing a variety of sexual horrors?"

I understood where the lieutenant was going when I answered. "Correct, sir."

"Will you explain to us how you ended up being televised since you were working an undercover operation?"

"Indeed, sir." I took a deep breath and licked my lips. "We knew the little girl was in the house and also knew a suspected killer was there, too. Sgt. Mora and his people were extremely professional while at the same time being leery of letting any other Mexican agency know of our operation. He arranged a standard professional forced entry into the house, clearly announcing that we were the police." I nodded in affirmation of my words. "Gatica was an incredibly brutal man. We knew his history, but our intention was to effect an arrest and rescue the child. Mr. Gatica could have surrendered, but chose not to."

"Did you shoot him?" the chief asked.

"No, sir. I didn't fire a shot. It was probably less than a minute later that we heard the Juarez City police coming with their sirens on. Sgt. Mora ran outside to head them off. I made sure the little girl was receiving proper care from a female officer who was with us, then I went outside. By that time, TV cameras were all over the place. I told the sergeant I was moving out, and I did. I made every reasonable effort not to be high profile, but I have to admit, it was a very chaotic scene. News crews, uniform cops, motor cops, an ambulance, even a fire truck." I shrugged. "I got the hell out of there and didn't go back."

I took a deep breath and sat back, sweat trickling down my collar. The sound of the door opening caught my attention. It was the control officer from the reception area. He stepped around me and went to the head of the table, leaned over, and whispered into the chief's ear.

The chief took a deep breath, waved off the officer, and looked at me with icy cold eyes. "You have a call. Officer Bustamante will show you to a private office. It's the president of the United States, and he wants to talk to you."

My heart pounded as I followed Bustamante out the door and to an office across the hall. I instantly understood its purpose. The walls and ceiling were acoustical tiles, the floor carpeted, and a heavy wooden desk was against the back wall with an executive chair pushed to the side. There were two telephones on the desk— one black, the other white. A note pad and a tray of pens and pencils were placed toward the back of the desk. An overhead panel of fluorescent bulbs provided soft, indirect lighting. It was a discreet conference room, free from outside eyes and ears.

Bustamante stepped halfway in, then moved aside and pointed toward the phones. "It's the white one," he said before he exited and closed the door.

I froze for a moment. Was I supposed to stand at attention when the president talked to me, or could I be seated? *What the hell, I* thought, *don't be so stupid.* I took a seat in the executive chair, was briefly tempted to put my feet up on the desk, then lifted the receiver. There was a momentary click before a strong male voice came on. "Officer Basurto, this is the president."

I responded, "Yes, sir, this is Officer Basurto, and thank you for calling."

"Nonsense, young man, *thank you"* he emphasized, "for the exceptional work you do protecting our borders and for the work you and your colleagues on both sides of the border did in rescuing that young child. I want you to know, Officer Basurto, that all of us here in the White House salute you, as do the members of Congress who have already spoken publicly this morning about your heroic deeds."

"Thank you, Mr. President, I appreciate your and everyone else's thoughts, but it's not just me. It's all of us. I simply happened to be in the right spot at the right time."

The president chuckled. "You're a humble man, Officer Basurto but, whether you realize it or not, you are a model of everything that is right in this great country. My wife and I wish Godspeed to you and those who work alongside you." He chuckled again and continued. "Ricky, if I may call you that, I personally hold you in high esteem for the work you do. And, Ricky," he laughed again, "if you ever get up this way, stop by and say hello."

I bit my lip and smiled inwardly. "Thank you, sir, and please know we respect and thank you for the great service you provide to us every day."

"Thanks, Ricky." He paused for a moment. "I must confess, the secretary told me you go by Ricky, and I consider you as my friend, so thanks, Ricky."

The phone clicked off. I held it for a moment and just looked at it—the president of the United States. Icy shivers coursed through my body. I took a deep breath, hung up, and went to the door. The hallway was empty. I opened the door to the conference room, but it was empty.

I caught myself smiling. The inquisition was over. I went back to the anteroom and found Miguel and Oscar thumbing through old magazines. They looked up when I opened the door, both politely holding back their broad grins.

"*Vamos,*" the lieutenant said when he started toward the exit. Miguel and I followed behind as he walked toward his marked patrol vehicle. He unlocked it, then turned around with a subdued guffaw. "Ricky, I was about to pee my pants in there. I had no idea the president would call, but I was positive you'd come out smelling like a rose. I've worked with the chief for years, and he's a hell of a good bureaucrat and gets a lot of good things done." He shook his head and looked down before continuing, "He doesn't have a nickel's worth of interpersonal skills, and hates like hell to have anybody getting publicity in the news—good or bad. He doesn't like it. I'm sorry you had to hear his bullshit, but that's him." Oscar laughed again. "But he never had the president call his hand."

Miguel tapped the fob to his car, gave me a joking salute, and commented, "Officer Basurto, do you have any work to do?"

"Yep," I said as I turned toward my pickup, "a lot of it."

CHAPTER THIRTEEN

I sent a text message to the Gonzaleses' lawyer with the approval to complete the asylum papers. He sent a quick reply, "*Gracias.*"

I sat for a few seconds in the Border Patrol parking lot and enjoyed the moment—the Gonzales family was doing okay, Muncie and I had a general plan for our lives, and the Salinas brothers might or might not be off the hook. Last, but not least, would be my personal project with Tony Castenada.

Anna messaged me with a smiley emoji and a note—a volunteer organization had placement for the Gonzales family near Deming. She sent a second note, "See u n a bit."

An hour later, I sat at my desk preparing documentation for my next step in the investigation on the Salinas brothers. My data entry was nearly complete when Anna popped in. I had never seen her so cheery. Her eyes were bright and sparkly. A smile revealed her perfect white teeth and I realized how gorgeous she was.

She pulled up a chair next to me, folded her arms over her chest, and gave a strong exhale. "Success," was all she said before she leaned over to my computer screen and gave a small guffaw. "But life continues, doesn't it? So where are we with those two jerks?"

"I'm running them through EPIC, and Mora is running all the Salinas names through their systems." I gave a half-hearted chuckle. "No sense trying to hide it anymore. They know we're on the hunt, and they'll do whatever serves them—including killing someone.

"He started with the *Centro Nacional de Inteligencia*, the CNI," I continued. "He also sent queries to the *Policia Federal Material*, the PFM. Truthfully, we don't expect much so we won't be disappointed with whatever comes back."

"If we don't give it a try," Anna said, "we would be neglecting potential information, so he's doing the right thing." She sat back and smiled again. "Now let me tell you where we are with the Gonzales family."

I scooted my chair around, crossed my legs, and sipped my lukewarm cup of coffee. "Good news, please," I implored.

"The nuns guided me to *Amigos Sin Fronteras* in Lordsburg. I called Mungia and turned it over to him. He talked to them, then called me back. I couldn't believe my ears," she joked. "*Amigos* had recruited a new host employer who wanted more than most hosts allow—an entire family. Generally, a host might take a single or a pair, but this was almost too much to hope for. It's a place called the Montenegro Agriculture Complex, south of Deming."

"Yeah, I know the place. Been by it a million times over the years. It's huge."

"That's an understatement. It's a year-round operation. They grow melons, onions, chilies, hay," she said while counting them off on her fingertips, "and a variety of smaller crops. Mungia told me the men will work in the fields, and the kid's mom, Abril, will cook for the farmhands—two meals a day, six days a week. Their salary will include modest housing, and the kids can go to school in Deming. Also on the positive side, they'll have an immigration hearing within the next twenty-four months." She smiled again. "With the workload in the courts, that's better than average. It's amazing."

She paused for a moment, frowned, and bit her lip. "The world isn't perfect. Catalina hasn't done well. The doctors believe she's suicidal, so they've admitted her to Desert Vista Behavioral Health Center in Alamogordo."

"Not good," I said.

"It gets worse. Alamogordo is one hundred fifty miles from the farm, so the poor kid is going to find herself bereft of family. They might be able to see her on weekends if someone takes them, otherwise...zilch, *nada*. She'll have to face it alone."

I gave a deep sigh. Their troubles weren't over, but they were off to a better-than-expected start in their new life. Catalina would be in their prayers.

Anna looked at her watch, then at me. "It's Saturday, which means it's supposed to be my day off." She cracked a grin, "Remember? I'm off Saturday and Sunday and, if you ever take a day off, it's supposed to be Sundays and Mondays. "*¿Recuerda?*" She looked over her shoulder as she walked out, "See you Tuesday."

I turned back to my PC. It was time for the Salinas family. I sent three sets of inquiries to EPIC, although my basic data was almost non-existent.

Alberto Salinas—20s, Chihuahua, Mexico; Federico Salinas—20s, Chihuahua, Mexico; Nicolas Salinas—50s, Chihuahua, Mexico. I looked at the screen. Paltry didn't describe it, but I didn't have anything else—at least for now.

* * *

It was time to shift gears. What would we find in the marijuana? The two bundles we recovered at the time of arrests were packed in a traditional custom backpack style—cellophane bricks wrapped tightly in a burlap bag and duct-taped shut. One or two belts were wrapped around it with sufficient length for the mule to strap it over his shoulders and carry it on his back.

I prepared a Request for Laboratory Analysis form and submitted it to the crime lab. The examination would be two-part: analysis to provide forensic evidence of the contents of the load; and an inspection of the cellophane-wrapped bricks for trace evidence (fingerprints and DNA) to match with the known samples we had of Oscar Davila and Ignacio Yanez.

I submitted an attachment suggesting more names and identifying data might be forthcoming for additional comparisons.

I submitted my requests via email to the laboratory, then sat back and looked at the ceiling. How was I going to get fingerprints or DNA from the Salinas brothers? If I could do that, then we might find a match on the marijuana bricks—maybe.

* * *

I let out a deep breath. There was no end to a case once it has been started—the damned tunnel. It needed to be eliminated *pronto*, not later.

Two hours and four phone calls later, Lt. Espinosa and Sgt. Mora met O'Rourke and me at the *El Jinete* for a late lunch in

Columbus. We ate with a minimum of conversation, then hurried to the tunnel. Daylight was slipping away in the western sky, and we needed to develop a plan. O'Rourke had already reviewed the land records with the county assessor and determined the parcel of interest was state-owned land, making it easier for us.

We traveled in O'Rourke's and my truck, speeding west on Hwy. 9 to a point a quarter-mile east of Julian Wash. I led the trek south across the desert until we came to our now *usual* mesquite tree on the knoll. This was where the case began, and we were eager to close it—in more ways than one.

* * *

"Shall we?" Mora quipped when he directed his old Kel-Lite beam into the mouth of the tunnel. I gave a quick wisecrack, "Who's older, you or your Kel-Lite?" then pulled my Streamlite Stinger from my belt and gave a serious, "*Vamonos.*"

I sat on my butt and slipped down into the tunnel. It was smaller than I expected—roughly four feet wide and five feet high. It would be a challenge to carry a fifty-pound pack, hunched over for a few hundred yards from end to end. I moved forward slowly with Sergio behind me. The tunnel was compact—walls and ceiling firm, the rock-solid floor evidence of numerous trips back and forth.

Profitable son of a bitch, I thought. *How many trips? How much a load? Marijuana or what? Pricks made a ton of greenbacks.*

Treading slowly and examining every bit of the tunnel, we reached the end ten minutes later. I pushed aside the plywood cover and hoisted myself up into a sitting position on the lip of the tunnel and in the State of Chihuahua.

Sergio pushed my legs aside and climbed up beside me. "*Chingue su madre,*" he uttered. "Out of sight of your million-dollar Border Patrol cameras?"

I nodded.

He continued. "Amigo, we've got work to do. Every day we're late, the Salinas people are going to the Church of the Holy Cash Register."

I lay back with my feet down in the tunnel. The sky was a deepening blue with a full moon peaking over the horizon. "You know what we need right now?" I inquired.

Sergio laughed. "A shovel."

"Nope, a six-pack," I joked.

* * *

It was that time of day when the coyotes began their mournful wail—first somewhere west of us, moments later another cry to the east. Then, as though responding to the symphony director, coyotes throughout the desert joined the lonesome call. Goosebumps crawled down my arms. I had heard this yowl hundreds of times over the years, but tonight was different. Their somber wail echoed as a funeral dirge across the desert. People's lives lay in the balance of whatever we did from this moment on.

* * *

We began the process the next morning of filling the tunnel with concrete in a coordinated operation with the Chihuahua State Engineers conducting their end of the operation.

O'Rourke and I oversaw a crew from *Roca Negra Hormigón* in New Mexico, directing a convoy of cement trucks across the desert to the northern terminus of the tunnel. In a slow, tedious process, six trucks emptied their nine-cubic-yard loads into the ground, while the Mexicans completed a similar function from their end.

It had been a grungy day by the time the last truck shifted into low gear and began the trek back to the highway. The tunnel was closed from both ends. Nobody would use it again.

I waited in my pickup for the dust to clear and watched O'Rourke trail behind the last empty truck when a thought hit me—the aspen grove.

Where's next?

CHAPTER FOURTEEN

S unday, and I took the day off. It was long overdue after working twelve days straight. Mom and I picked up Rosalinda in
time for Mass in Mesilla, then on to brunch at Café Obregon on
the square.

It was a grand day with the women I love: a beautiful service
in the historic Basilica de San Albino, a meal fit for royalty in the
café, and an afternoon shopping in the *tiendas* and boutiques on
the square and the kiosks in the park.

The one thing we didn't do was discuss work—neither
Muncie's nor mine.

* * *

The shadows of the Big Hatchet Mountains were creeping across
la bajada by the time we left Rosalinda at her apartment. The day

had been one of those rare times when life was everything it was supposed to be: peaceful, spiritual, and filial. I felt young again.

Having a day off does not necessarily mean work is totally out of mind. The brightly painted number fifteen glared at me from the trestle as we cruised west on Hwy. 9.

Thirty minutes later, we approached the dirt road leading from the highway to our house. Goosebumps zipped through my arms and legs when we saw what lay ahead. Mom leaned forward against her seat belt and peered out the windshield. *"¿Qué paso?"* Her voice was nearly inaudible.

My eyes darted back and forth between Momma and the State Police car blocking the road to our house. Something was wrong. Very wrong. Nervous energy stormed through every muscle of my body as I raced the final quarter-mile to our driveway. I hit the brakes when I pulled onto the dirt shoulder, skidding to a halt alongside the patrol car. A quick pang of guilt swarmed over me as a cloud of dust enveloped us and the trooper who was exiting his car.

Pushing my door open, I issued a quick apology to the trooper— Karl Mueller, a graduate of my rookie class. "Carlos," I said, using the nickname we hung on him in the Academy. "I'm sorry about the dirt. What's happening? This is my Mom's and my house."

Pulling off his dirty sunglasses, he answered. "Ricky, we've been looking for you the last couple of hours." He turned to my mother as she was getting out of the truck. *"Lo siento, pero."*

Mother raised her hand incisively, stopping the young trooper in mid-sentence. Her expression was stoic, but polite. "I speak English, Mr. Mueller. Yes, I understand there is a problem, but tell me what happened."

"A fire, Mrs. Basurto. Trooper Benavidez spotted the smoke and went up there. It's bad."

"Thanks," I said, swallowing my heart in my mouth. Directing Mom to get in the truck, I jumped behind the wheel, went around Karl's vehicle, and up the dirt road to our home. We saw the burned-out rubble as we crested the last knoll before the house. There was nothing left.

Momma broke into tears. I choked mine back, but my mind was in a whirl. All our history was gone—letters, pictures, knick-knacks, clothes, the little things that make up daily life—all destroyed. Only the chicken coop remained untouched by the flames.

My government pickup truck had been parked at the west side of the house. They had trashed it—tires cut, windows broken out, and the seat slashed to pieces, but it hadn't burned. Mom's old Chevy was parked near the chicken coop, untouched.

I saw a firefighter at the back of the rubble, working his K-9 through our burned-out home.

Lt. Sosa and Benavidez approached as Mom and I got out, our eyes glued on the destruction of our home, the front porch where we had coffee at sunrise today, the porch we rested on in the evening and listened to the coyotes and their bone-chilling cry.

"I'm sorry, Ricky," Sosa said, then turned to Mom, "I'm very sorry, Mrs. Basurto." He motioned to his car and continued, "Let's have a seat and we can tell you what we know."

"No, I'll stand," Mom said as she leaned back against my truck.

"Momma..." I looked into her tear-swollen eyes, "Momma, you'll be more comfortable in the lieutenant's car."

She glared momentarily at Sosa, then back to the remains of her home. "I want to stand."

The lieutenant gestured to Benavidez. "Go over it with them."

The young trooper stood erect, almost at attention, then directed his comments to us. "I was working traffic on I-10, and some on Route 146 toward Hachita. I was exactly 2.4 miles south of the

Interstate when I saw an SUV northbound—fast, very fast." The trooper paused to wipe the sweat from his brow and lick his lips, then continued. "I clocked him at 104 miles per hour." He cracked a hint of a smile and nodded approval of his comments. "He was coming toward me, so I flicked on my overheads and he backed off immediately. He was slowing when he passed me, so I whipped around and stopped him a little further north. It was two men, the driver and a younger guy. They were all right, very polite and apologetic, 'just blowing out the exhaust,' they said. I ran records on both of them and the SUV. Everything checked 10-4."

Benavidez shrugged his shoulders. "I wrote the guy a ticket, and they went on their way."

"Who were they?" I asked.

Benavidez pulled his notebook from his pocket and thumbed through it for a second. Nodding his head, he read aloud the names and identifiers of the two men, "Federico Alberto Salinas; he's forty-two years old, lives in Seminole, Texas, and owns the vehicle, a 2018 Lexus GX-460, silver in color. His passenger was Hector Gonzales Moreno. He's twenty-nine and lives in Brownfield, Texas. They're cousins and were down here to meet another cousin in Animas, but he didn't show, or so they say."

"Who were they supposedly meeting with?" Sosa asked.

Benavidez shuffled his feet, looked down, and kicked aimlessly at a stone. "I wish I had separated them, but I didn't have any reason to think anything was wrong—just heavy on the gas." He paused and shook his head. "They said a cousin from Chihuahua was coming up to see about buying some horses, but he never showed, so they left. Then I stopped them. End of story."

"Cousin's name?" I asked.

Benavidez shook his head and looked at his feet. "I didn't ask."

Sosa interjected, "Go on. Tell them about the fire."

The young trooper took a moment to collect his thoughts, and then continued. "I hadn't been down Hwy. 146 all day, so I just cruised south. It's beautiful but treacherous country. Banditos, coyotes, immigrants, you name it and it's there. I was getting close to Hachita when I smelled smoke, but I couldn't see anything and you can see forever down here. I drove to the general store and got out of my car, and *really* smelled the smoke, but didn't know where it was coming from. I got a Dilly Bar and asked Marta—she's the clerk—and she smelled it, too, but didn't know where the source was.

"Anyhow, I got back in my unit and came east on Hwy. 9. That's when I spotted some smoke up here. I came up the drive but, by the time I got here, the house had collapsed. It was gone. I called it in on my radio. It took forever, but the Volunteer Fire Department finally got here. There wasn't much they could do except douse the ashes."

Sosa spoke. "I had one of the Sheriff's units go to Animas to determine if we could verify the story Salinas told Benavidez about being there to meet someone. They called me back and more or less validated it—a couple guys in a light-colored SUV stopped in the café, had some chow and coffee. They seemed to be stalling for something, then they left. The people at the café didn't see them meet anyone, but also they can't say they didn't."

"How does their time fit the timeframe of our fire?" I asked.

"He," the lieutenant said with a shrug toward Benavidez, "wrote the ticket at 3:05, then called in the fire at four o'clock on the button. The deputy said they were in Animas around two or two-thirty, give or take a little. So, to answer your question, they fit fairly well."

We turned our attention to the firefighter and his dog as they stepped around the last pieces of burned material and approached us. His yellow duckbill overalls were grimy with soot and mud, and his face similarly dirty from scratching through what was left of our home. The dog, a Belgian Malinois, wore protective rubber boots. His tan hair, like his handler's, was covered in mud and soot.

"I think we've got it," he said to Sosa, then looked at Mom and me. "I'm Chief Hamilton with the Volunteer Fire Co-op. The guys who put the flames down left an hour ago, but I always follow up to ascertain the cause of the fire." Looking down at his dog who was sitting at his feet, he said, "Bingo hit on three separate spots— definitely an accelerant was used. It's an old house, and went up in a hurry." He looked to Mom and me and continued. "Mighty sorry, folks. We'll send some burned samples in to the crime lab. They'll let us know what was used, but I'm going to guess right now. It was nothing special, just gasoline."

He looked at me and continued, "You're a cop, right?"

I nodded. "State Police."

"Well, I figure you probably wouldn't have a gas can in the house, would you?"

I shook my head. "No, why?"

"Whoever did this started in the rear bedroom. My guess is they hit the front bedroom next, then dumped the last of their gas in the main room along with the can. They likely got the hell out 'cause it was going up in a hurry."

He took a deep breath, reached down and patted Bingo's ears, and continued. "There ain't nothing for us to get fingerprints or trace evidence from. It's all just burned to hell."

Momma's bedroom, I thought. *Rotten bastards.*

I turned at the sound of traffic coming up our road. The first was O'Rourke's black GMC Tahoe, followed by Muncie in her car, then her dad behind her.

In one way, I felt completely lost but, in another, just seeing friends and family gave me a warm glow. I looked at Momma, put my arm around her waist, and pulled her close. We were a family and would get through this.

Rosalinda ran to Mom and wrapped her in her arms, then turned to me and pulled me in.

Miguel drove by my trashed-out pickup, got out and shook his head, then walked over to us. He joined us, and I had to give a little laugh. A group hug wasn't very macho.

After all the comforting comments, Rosalinda and I stepped aside to talk privately. "Ricky, Miguel called me as soon as he got the information, and I called Lupe in Denver. I told her we'd call her later when we have some details." She lowered her chin and shook her head. "She's really worried about your mom. Do you have any fallback plans?"

"Zilch."

"I didn't think so, but Daddy and I talked and came up with an idea. It's not long-range, but will do for starters. Why don't you and your mother make a Target run to Deming? Get enough stuff for about a week—whatever you need to hold you over. She can stay with my parents. Their house is huge, and she won't be in their way." She cupped my face in her hands and spoke softly. "Stay at my place. At least for now until things can be worked out."

I shook my head. "Hmm, I don't know. It might be awkward."

Rosalinda gave a wisp of a giggle. "For her or for you?"

CHAPTER FIFTEEN

Clearing our property was tedious but necessary. Mom, Lupe, and I spent a fruitless day grubbing through the debris searching for anything of personal or monetary value. In the end, we were filthy and empty-handed.

I didn't know time could go so fast, but it did. Lupe took Mom to live with them in Denver, temporarily at least. I moved my new but meager belongings into Rosalinda's apartment in Columbus, and the insurance adjuster settled for a paltry $36,000 for our home and its contents.

I tried to divorce myself from work but was only partially successful. I let go of the Gonzales family, couldn't care less about who or what was being smuggled across the border and cared even less about the flood of human beings pouring over the international boundary to surrender for amnesty.

The duty roster listed me *on vacation* but it was deceiving. Our little family was struggling to put our lives back together again.

Two weeks after our day from hell, Rosalinda and I drove to Santa Fe for a family meeting. We drove up Saturday afternoon and met Mom along with Lupe and her husband, Daniel, for a casual dinner. Later, we had a long family discussion in the privacy of Lupe and Daniel's suite at the Hotel Santa Rita. Mom was adamant. She would not leave Hachita. She was born there, and had every intention of dying there, preferably of natural causes but, if at the hands of the cartel, then so be it.

We would rebuild. We accepted Mom's wishes—board-and-batten construction similar to what we had, with two bedrooms, a bathroom, and a great room—a near-replica to the floor plan of the original house.

Sunday morning we gathered for Mass at the Basilica of Saint Francis of Assisi. It was a glorious day, not unlike two weeks ago, with a blessed church service, brunch at the Bull Ring, followed by hugs and kisses before our departures—a long drive north for them and one south for us.

* * *

Rosalinda took me to work Monday morning. After all the condolences and greetings, Anna and I adjourned for coffee in the employee lounge where she briefed me on the activities I had missed.

The Gonzales family had settled into their new life on the Montenegro farm, but Catalina was still institutionalized in Alamogordo. I nodded. That was exactly what I expected, but it seemed Anna was doing a slow song-and-dance routine. Why was she dawdling, just making busy conversation to be talking?

Nevertheless, she continued rambling. The DEA had a clean, late model vehicle for my new company car, and it would be delivered later this morning by El Paso personnel. She was sure it was something I'd like.

I nodded again with a semi-tart comment, "That's nice."

Suddenly, it hit me. She was building up her own nerve to broach something, but what? We had been in the break room for ten minutes, but no one else had come in. Finally, I leaned across the table angrily. "Spit it out, Anna. What the fuck is going on?"

She pulled back in her chair as tears streamed down her cheeks. "They killed Sergio." She took a deep breath, moistened her lips, and continued. "Not just him. His girlfriend, too."

My reaction was spontaneous. Lying forward on the table, I buried my face in my hands and cried. *Oh God, not Sergio. Please,* I prayed.

"It was Friday night," Anna continued. "They had been at a *Quinceañera* in Juarez. They left just a couple of minutes before it happened. Sergio had stopped at a traffic light when they were hit with automatic weapons fire." She took another deep breath and dabbed her eyes with a tissue. "At least the cartel didn't kidnap and torture them. They died instantly and didn't have to suffer."

I sat up straight, caught my breath, and got a bottle of water from the refrigerator. My mind was in a whirl. "Okay," I said. "Any more surprises for me?"

She bit her lips and shook her head. "I don't think so, but Oscar Pineda is coming over with your new ride from El Paso, and he's got some info for you." She shrugged her shoulders. "I don't have any idea what it is."

* * *

I was sitting on a bench beneath the ramada on the shady side of our building when two vehicles pulled into our parking lot, a black Highlander and a Corvette. I still had it in me to give a little chuckle. The Corvette wasn't for me.

Recognizing Oscar from some previous briefings, I walked toward him when he got out of the Highlander. A big man, always wearing western garb, he strode in my direction while signaling for his partner to come along.

I gestured in the direction of the ramada, and they followed along. We each pulled up lawn chairs while Oscar introduced me to Felicia Ortega, his undercover partner. We exchanged pleasantries, then Oscar leaned over with his elbows on his knees. Felicia sat back in stoic silence.

"Amigo," he said. "You and Sergio bit off a big chew. That Matagente asshole was expendable, but the cartel is *really* pissed, not so much about losing him, but more so about losing their tunnel." He sat back, crossed his leg over his knee and continued. "Apparently that tunnel had been a gold mine for them and now it's gone." He grimaced and gave a Cheshire cat grin. "You guys screwed them big time, so somebody had to pay. I've got a snitch that's close to *La Linea*, and they're the group that hit Sergio. For a price, of course."

Oscar lit a cigarette, took a deep inhale, and continued. "You might find this strange, but they figure the debt is paid. They killed a Mexican on his home turf but didn't want to kill a Yankee cop north of the border. They figured it would cause too much trouble, and they're right. So they hit your house. They knew no one was home so there would be no murder rap, but they delivered their message. It's this, we know you and everything about you, so stay on your side of the border.

"Ricky, you're a good cop, but these guys aren't playing games.

119

If I was you, I'd stay on our side of the line. It's not worth it even to go to Palomas for lunch." He shook his head. "You can do your job here, but don't go down there for anything."

Felicia, who had been sitting quietly, rose from her chair and pulled it alongside Oscar. "I had been working your guy, Matagente, for a couple of months. On background, we think he may have been involved in some killings in Arizona and quite a few further south in Mexico." She smiled softly. "I believe he was long overdue. It was just a matter of time before somebody hit him.

"I'm sorry about Sgt. Mora and his friend. Her name was Alicia Gonzales: no relation to the family you worked." She bit her lip and frowned. "I just don't like us to talk about crime victims as if they were some inanimate objects. She had a name, and we need to call her by it." She folded her arms over her chest. "Sergeant Sergio Mora and Alicia Gonzales. She was a single mother with a two-year-old daughter. The child is Maria, and she's been taken in by her grandparents."

She closed her eyes, sighed, and gave a grim smile. "Now I feel better."

CHAPTER SIXTEEN

Tuesday started better than Monday. The bank loan was approved, the contractor was ready to start the job, and an ecstatic Lupe had called at the crack of dawn. She was pregnant.

There was something I had learned as a combat Marine: Regardless of the situation, always have a Plan B. Fortunate for us, we had one, and it was up and running. We would have a new home by the end of summer; my mind was clear on what I had to do with Tony Castenada and the Salinas family, and our wedding date was set: November 30th.

Sitting in my office cubicle, I opened my computer and was greeted with the EPIC information on the Salinas family. Their response was short and to the point:

The El Paso Information Center finds nothing to clearly identify Alberto and Federico Salinas. The full name for Nicolas Salinas is Rodrigo Nicolas Salinas, but he is generally known as Nicolas. His occupation is that of a cattle importer. He has had and still has a multi-year contract with the Secretariat of National Defense to supply beef for the Army and the Navy.

Background data indicate his sons, Alberto and Federico, serve as purchasing agents for the family business, legally named Chihuahua Land and Cattle, S.A., also known as *Chihuahua Tierra y Ganado, S.A.*

The family business is located in Ascension Municipality, but the financial matters are transacted in Mexico City, Mexico.

There is no identifiable information to connect the business or Rodrigo Nicolas Salinas to any criminal enterprise.

* * *

I had held out that something, however minuscule, might surface but wasn't surprised by what I had learned. On the opposite side of this blank coin was the cold, hard fact that there would be nothing coming from Sgt. Mora's inquiries. All it had done was to seal his death warrant.

I took what little we had on the Salinas men and met with Acacia in her office. Working with my meager information, she assured me she would search databases that are normally outside the parameters of EPIC. Her unique techniques allowed her to search city and county jurisdictions for misdemeanor offenses, something that was beyond most Fusion Center search zones. She would focus on jurisdictions with a common boundary or a near-common boundary with Mexico. As she explained it, there was always a potential for an insignificant run-in with the law that didn't reach the levels necessary for documentation in criminal history or criminal intelligence files. If the Salinas faction, especially the two young men, ventured into Texas, New Mexico, Arizona, or California, their known tendencies for aggressive behavior may have put them in contact with law enforcement. If that had occurred, there was the possibility of fingerprints or other identifying data to be on file.

Acacia politely ended our conversation as she had done previously, "And don't ask me when I'll get it done. You'll be the first to know."

* * *

There was something deep within my soul—one last arrow in my quiver that I had not yet shot: Tony Castenada. Was he targeted by Matagente? Or, at least, was he actually my mother's uncle who was killed during an undercover drug operation? I knew I had no official government purpose to pursue this, but I was going to do whatever was necessary to learn about it once and for all. It was too close to home to simply let it go. I had to know.

I checked my personnel files and found I had accumulated sixty hours of compensatory time, hours I would not be paid for but could use at my discretion.

This was my discretion.

I met with O'Rourke and shared the unusual coincidence about Mom's uncle. Like me, he was taken aback. It was a twist of fate that two of us so closely related and in the same business could have these close encounters with the same person, Julian Espino Gatica, 6-6-6. Satan personified.

"Take your days," he said. "But, by damn, I want to know how this comes out. This is too uncanny for both of you to be dealing with that same crazy bastard."

I repeated Acacia's comments as I went out the door, "Don't ask. You'll be the first to know."

The next hour was spent winnowing through the Tucson Police Department assistant chiefs, captains, and lieutenants until I finally connected with Lt. Kevin Kaminski of the Special Intelligence section. Our brief conversation was gold.

"Yeah, sure," he said. "It was before my time here on the PD, but his name is on the memorial out front."

The deal was sealed. I would be in Tucson Thursday morning.

* * *

After dinner, Muncie and I strolled to the apartment's common area, carrying a bottle of her favorite Pinot Grigio, *Collio Schiopetto*. It was a quiet sanctuary where only the gurgling sound of the fountain and the cooing of the mourning doves broke the serenity of the early evening. We could not have selected a more tranquil place—sidewalks bordered with an array of wildflowers, the sweet scent of tangerine and orange trees, and a soft breeze sweeping the long-familiar smells of the desert across our little heaven on earth.

Appropriately, we found a loveseat tucked beneath a towering eucalyptus tree. I poured the wine, looked into her beautiful green eyes, and spoke. "Muncie, there's something I need to tell you…"

Before I could continue, she arched her back and shifted forward on the bench, an expression of bewilderment scrawled across her face. "Ricky, no more. I can't handle any more bad news." She shook her head, looked down at her feet, then stared into my eyes. "Please, Ricky. I can't handle it."

I put my arms around her waist and pulled her into me. "Muncie, no. It's nothing bad, I promise." I cracked a smile and kissed her cheek. "It's something I need to do, but nothing to worry about. It's just a question I need to put to rest. It's personal, but both of us will be glad to have it behind us."

She sat back and twisted around to face me, dubious, but willing to hear me out.

"I never told you about Mom's Uncle Tony, did I?"

She shook her head, and I told her the story—all of it. Tony Castenada, Reynaldo Guzman, Mary Elizabeth Martin, Julian Espino Gatica and his alias, Matagente.

The sun had set before we finished our talk. I was leaving in the morning and meeting with Tucson staff on Thursday morning. "By the time I come home, I'll know the complete story of Antonio Castenada, of Guzman and Martin and, most of all, the story of Matagente."

We clinked our now-empty glasses and walked hand in hand to *our* apartment. There was no need for dinner. We simply inhaled each other in pure, emotional love. Her soft, beautiful breasts, her gorgeous bottom, and the indescribable taste of the woman I loved.

CHAPTER SEVENTEEN

I drove into Tucson after a pleasant six-hour drive across I-10. It was two o'clock, which gave me ample time to scout the area, particularly Police Headquarters on Stone Ave. I exited the freeway onto the Congress St. off-ramp, turned right, then another right, and I was there—the place where my granduncle served his community, and where he gave his life.

I found a bit of humor in spite of the serious purpose of my trip. Antonio Castenada, my mother's uncle. How were we related? It was beyond my comprehension, so Rosalinda explained it to me. It helped that her hobby was the study of ancestry, so my question was a no-brainer for her. Mom's uncle was my granduncle or, some would say, my great uncle. "Both," she said, "are accurate."

I found the police department to be housed in a modern building with a Memorial Plaza facing the thoroughfare. I did a slow drive-by and was surprised by how they memorialized their fallen. It was overwhelming. I drove around the block, then slipped into the parking lot and walked through the plaza to experience the passion of its meaning.

An expansive area, the plaza consisted of an upright, white marble stone that was the original monument. To that, and in recognition of the city's 250-year history, they placed another monument upon which an early era hat, badge, gun belt, holster, and six-shooter hung as though on a nail by the door. On the front side of the monolith rested a bronze casting of a woman releasing a dove from her fingertips. A bronze K-9 sat at her feet.

Adjacent to it laid an immense black granite open book with the names of the fallen inscribed on its open pages, dating back to 1892.

Stepping to the book, I found my granduncle, Antonio Castenada. We had come full circle. I would carry his memory throughout my life and pass it on to the children yet to be born to Rosalinda and me.

* * *

At exactly ten o'clock Thursday morning, I was at the front entrance of the Tucson Police Department. For the briefest moment, my mind jumped back to the history of my Thursdays. They were bad memories. Hopefully, this Thursday would break the mold.

With my fingers crossed, I displayed my badge and identification card to the uniformed woman at the front counter. She carefully examined my documents, then waved me through with a pleasant, "Please be seated. Someone from the chief's office will be down momentarily."

I was seated only seconds before footsteps on the flagstone

stairwell drew my attention. It was a young officer, his uniform creased and starched, coming toward me. "Officer Basurto?" he asked. I rose and met him at the bottom of the stairs. After brief introductions, I followed him to the elevator, then down the hall to the chief's conference room. Suddenly, the reality of the moment struck me. My own flesh and blood had worked in this building, and today we would rekindle his life as a Tucson police officer.

I was surprised when we entered the conference room. It was overflowing with uniform and plainclothes officers, department brass, undercover male and female officers displaying their badges on their belts or lanyards draped around their necks, and a mature, professionally dressed woman with two cameras strapped around her neck and shoulders.

The chief, with four stars on her uniform collar, extended her hand as she stepped away from the refreshment tray. "Trooper Basurto, I'm Chief Hardyman. Welcome to Tucson." We shook hands, then the others came forward, shaking hands, and giving quick introductions. After a few minutes of polite chit-chat, coffee, and bagels, Chief Hardyman invited us to be seated. She sat at the head of the table and invited me to sit to her right.

The photographer moved about the room, adjusting her lenses, and taking photos. At her direction, the chief and I stood for a few moments while the camera clicked away.

Hardyman thanked her for the pictures and assured me she would send a couple to me in remembrance of today. Then she nodded in the direction of a solidly built, middle-aged man wearing a sports jacket and open-collar shirt. "Captain Willis, give us a synopsis of Detective Castaneda's tenure here at the PD."

"Yes, ma'am," he replied, then shifted his eyes to me. "Trooper, we're honored you would go to so much effort to learn more about your mother's uncle." He gave a soft chuckle and continued. "I had to Google it but, if I have it right, Detective Castenada was your granduncle."

I returned his smile. "Yes, sir. Granduncle or, some would say, great uncle."

He chuckled again, "I think we both had to do our homework." He paused, then continued somberly. "Detective Castenada was an outstanding officer and a gentleman. His career here started in the late '90s. He was married to a beautiful lady, Elizabeth Califano. They had two kids. Matthew and Mark.

"Tony, if you don't mind me calling him by that…"

"No, no," I interjected. "That's how I know him. Uncle Tony."

Willis nodded, then spoke again. "Our situation back then was probably similar to what you're experiencing in your current assignment, so we marshaled forces and formed a Task Force. It was us, the Sheriff's Department, DPS, DEA, and the county attorneys from Pima and Cochise Counties. Tony eventually developed an informant, a woman named Sara Hurtado. She had an on-again/off-again boyfriend named Reynaldo Guzman.

"Guzman was a wheeler and dealer. He owned a large vegetable import business in Nogales. Plus, being politically astute, he spent a lot of money backing political figures and donating to charitable causes. Overall, he was highly respected and associated with major politicians and financial gurus all over the state." Willis offered a half-hearted smirk. "Sex was his weakness, and that's how he met Sara. She was a working girl in a resort he frequented. He got friendly with her, and one thing led to another.

"The turning point came with a high profile murder case in the foothills west of town. They blew up an entire family—mom, dad, and kids. Sara had reason to believe Guzman was behind it and, to make a long story short, she gave her information to Tony.

"It took a few weeks, but Ms. Hurtado eventually introduced

him to Guzman as a long-lost relative. Of course, Guzman did her a favor and hired Tony into his legit business." Willis smirked again, then continued. "Tony was good at collecting debts, most likely from drug transactions for Guzman's shady business. Your granduncle eventually developed sufficient evidence to indict Guzman, his business accountant Mary Martin, and others for smuggling drugs from Sonora into Arizona.

"Detective Castenada did a magnificent job documenting every step of his investigation, creating a solid chain of evidence for everything he collected that could tie the Guzman organization to drug smuggling, and even kept meticulous internal records for his expenditures such as car mileage, food, and any other expenses he accrued.

"At some point, someone in the Guzman group decided Sara had squealed on them, so they kidnapped her and took her to the desert near Sasabe. That's where our common suspect, Matagente or, as we also know him, Julian Espino Gatica, tortured her. We believe she endured excruciating pain as was evidenced by her post-mortem, but eventually surrendered and gave up Tony. So," the captain let out a deep exhale. "our mutual enemy, Matagente, killed her with his .22 pistol. It wasn't long after that when they hit Tony. It happened in a parking garage a couple of blocks from where we are now—one .38 shot to the head.

"We never developed sufficient evidence, but we believe it was Mary Martin who actually pulled the trigger. Apparently, she had planned an affair with Detective Castenada. When she learned he was a cop, she took it as a personal offense and killed him." Willis leaned back as if composing himself, then continued. "Guzman and his associates had every high dollar lawyer this side of the Mississippi, and they went after Tony. Of course, he was our star witness, and his testimony would have been corroborated by Ms.

Hurtado. Unfortunately, both of them were dead and we couldn't move forward in court with only his documented evidence. Even if we tried, their lawyers had already brought in a couple of paid witnesses, and they shredded his reputation with every sickening lie you could imagine. In the end, there was no prosecution for his murder or the drug dealing. Everybody walked."

"Matagente?" I asked.

The chief interjected, "In a way, justice prevailed. Guzman and Mary Martin took up residence in his ranch house about halfway between here and Nogales. Within a couple of months of Detective Castaneda's death, an unidentified person shot and killed both of them as they sat in their hot tub—one shot to the head for each of them."

"Information came across the border from a snitch in Nogales that Gatica was the hitman." She shook her head, looked down, then continued. "It fits his M.O. He had a reputation for a .22 shot to the head as his calling card. That doesn't answer as to *why* someone had them wiped out, but everyone associated with the case tends to believe the Matagente theory was true. Nevertheless, not long after that, he dropped off the radar until you came along. Which brings us to the next point—you and Mr. Gatica. Was he a player in whatever you were investigating?"

"Yes, ma'am," I replied. "My partner and I were working with our Mexican counterparts when his name came up. Our intelligence unit believed he had a falling out with the Sinaloa Cartel, so he left Sonora and came to Chihuahua and the Juarez/La Linea Cartel.

"The Chihuahua State Police and I were investigating a child trafficking case. We had reliable information the little girl was being held at a specific house in Juarez. It was also established that Matagente was the *jefe* in charge of the place. We hit it late in the afternoon, and our information was correct. The youngster—her name is Catalina Gonzales—was stripped naked and tied down on a bed. Of course, Matagente was there, too.

"We conducted an announced forced entry, but Gatica came at us with a handgun. He didn't get more than a foot into the room before our officers shot him—six shots, center of mass. He never got a shot off, and it was over in no more than a second." I gave a soft, condescending chuckle. "His pea-shooter was a .22."

"Did the child survive?" the chief asked.

I nodded. "Indeed, but she's not doing well. She's been committed to a mental health unit in Alamogordo."

"I'm sorry to hear that, but at least the world will no longer have Mr. Gatica to cause us grief." She smiled as she took a piece of paper from her shirt pocket. "We took the opportunity to contact Mrs. Castenada. She's a dental hygienist and gets home around three o'clock." Handing the notepaper to me, she continued, "She would like to meet you. She wanted to be here but had to work. I told her you might contact her this afternoon." Pointing to her handwritten note, she said, "If you'd like, I can have someone take you there, or you can Google it. That's her phone number and address. It's about a thirty-minute drive from here. It's fairly close to where they lived before her husband was killed. She moved not long after his death, but is still in the same part of town—good schools, shopping, that sort of thing."

I nodded appreciatively and tucked the note into my pocket. "I'll give her a call and see her this afternoon. Google Maps will get me there, then tomorrow I'll get back to New Mexico." I paused for a quick thought, then spoke, "I'm curious. Coming through downtown, I saw a statue of Pancho Villa on horseback. My home is in Hachita, a few miles west of Columbus where my fiancé lives." I couldn't hold back my smile. "In history class, we learned Villa led the only army to ever invade the United States. He got as far as Columbus before he was chased back into Mexico. But, here, there's a statue of him in the middle of the government district." I shook my head. "I don't understand."

The chief chuckled. "We don't, either. It's been there since the early '80s. Every few years there's a movement to have it removed but, as you saw, it's still there. It's called *Viente de Agosto* Park. Obviously, we have a large Hispanic population. Some revere him as a hero; others consider him a thief and murderer. The rest of us just say it's a contradiction we live with."

When the meeting began to break up, an older, well-groomed, bearded man came from the back of the room. Offering his hand, he spoke softly. "Trooper Basurto, I'm Anthony Allbright. I worked with Tony back in the day." Taking my elbow, he spoke, "Can I walk you to your car?"

We walked in silence through the hall, down the elevator, and outside by the plaza before he uttered a word. Standing in the shade of a palm tree, Allbright smiled heartily, shaking his head.

"I never thought this day would come but, when I received an invitation to be here, I jumped at it. What you heard upstairs is true. Tony was a hell of a good cop and as honorable a man who ever wore a badge. What happened to him was wrong. Personally, though, what they did after they killed him was even worse—the shit they said about him."

He pulled a pack of Camels from his pocket and lit up. Giving a self-deprecating smirk, he said, "Another of their friggin' rules: no smoking." Taking a deep inhale and blowing it out his nose, he continued. "I've never said these words to another human in all these years, but hell, I'm eighty-one years old now, so what the fuck." He laughed aloud. "Hell, yes, I know who arranged for Guzman and his whore to get smoked. Lots of people in those days figured it out, but I knew from the start what was going to happen." Shaking his head, he continued his monologue. "All of us knew the bastards would get away with it, but there was something inside me that said otherwise. Besides that, when I was CIA, I worked in Central America dealing with Julian Gatica on several cases."

Allbright coughed until I thought his lungs were coming out, then spit on the grass. "Shit, I'm the man who put the tag on that son of a bitch—*Matagente*, the one who kills people. He was a killing bastard. I think he was part Aztec or Inca. Whatever he was, like in the frontier days in our own country, the Native Americans took coup to prove their bravery and skill. Matagente had his own way of taking coup. He used a .22, and that meant he had to be within an arm's length of his victim so he could guarantee a single shot to the brain would kill his target." Allbright shook his head in disgust and looked down at his shoes. "Most of the people he eliminated had it coming, but a few were as innocent as freshly fallen snow. It didn't make any difference to him. If he took the money, he did the job. That's one good thing you can say about him. He earned his pay each and every time."

I shook my head. "I'm not sure I'm following you."

He put his hands on my shoulders and looked into my eyes. "I liked Tony and couldn't let Guzman and his bitch get away with it. I planned it and met with that skinny prick, Gatica, for dinner in Guaymas. I won't say how I got the money, but I paid him half upfront and half after the deed was done." Shaking his head, he loosened his grip on me and inhaled. "I might go to hell for the life I've led, but killing that pair was the right thing to do."

He started to turn away, then stopped in mid-step. His face was that of a tired, old man. His eyes were tearing. "You take care of yourself."

CHAPTER EIGHTEEN

I sat in my pickup and watched Allbright meander across Stone Avenue to a parking lot crammed between two old and crumbling buildings. He stood beside a classic 1964 Corvette Stingray, stubbed out his cigarette, and slipped behind the wheel. Like a senior citizen, he eased out of the driveway, stopped for slow-moving traffic a block away, then drove south on Stone and disappeared.

A dinosaur, I thought, *but an essential element at the time.*

Turning on my air conditioning and radio, I had to laugh out loud. The DJ was also laughing—the temperature at eleven o'clock was 105 degrees, but it was a dry heat. That was supposed to make it feel cooler.

Retracing my route from the *Hotel Árbol de Sombra* this morning, I went east on Speedway Blvd. to Bread Winners Café for a cup of soup and a sandwich. Between bites of food, I checked my cellphone for directions to Mrs. Castenada's residence. I knew it was somewhere nearby but was surprised how close I was—the

900 block of Gadsden Place was only a couple of miles away from my hotel.

Knowing she worked and wouldn't be off until three o'clock, I took advantage of the leisure time. My minimal packing for the trip was sufficient. I had a swimming suit. An hour later, I was poolside at the hotel with an ice-cold *Modelo Chelada*. Life was good and I was looking forward to meeting my granduncle's wife.

Allowing for her to have time to come home and kick back, I waited until almost four o'clock before I called her. She answered on the first ring, as melodic a voice as I had ever heard.

Twenty minutes later, I was at her door—a single-story, burnt adobe home with a rock and cactus garden in the front yard. I was reaching for the doorbell when she opened the door: a stunning lady in her early fifties, dark hair with a few gray tendrils, wearing a white sleeveless blouse, khaki shorts, and sandals. She was nothing less than elegant.

"Good afternoon, Mr. Basurto," she remarked as she moved aside and gestured for me to come in.

I stepped inside and was welcomed with the cool touch of her air conditioning. It was already up to 109 degrees according to the radio station I was listening to.

"Mrs. Castenada," I said, "I'm so honored to meet you." I gave a light chortle. "I'm not sure how we're related. I know your husband was my granduncle," I laughed again, "so maybe you're my grandaunt."

I followed her into the family room with a view over her patio and swimming pool.

"Have a seat," she said, "while I find us something to drink. I have beer, wine, or tea. Your preference?"

"Same as you're having."

She gave a soft laugh. "Its *Cerveza* time in the Old Pueblo."

I took a glance around the open area of a family room, dining room, and kitchen. It was as elegant as she—a Talavera tile floor, open beam ceiling, a painting of *El Santuario de Chimayo* over the fireplace, and a matching sofa, loveseat, and chair gathered around a heavy dark wood coffee table.

I sat on the sofa with a view of the pool and the mountains in the background. The ambiance was soothing, yet homey. By all appearances, she had done well with her life.

Mrs. Castenada was behind the kitchen counter. "Iced mug?" she asked. She didn't wait for a response before she came in carrying a frothy mug in each hand.

I rose, accepted one, then touched our mugs together, "To our long-lost relationship."

She smiled the most beautiful smile in the world, second only to my Muncie.

She sat on the love seat, and I returned to the sofa. "Mr. Basurto," she said, "we're much too formal. My maiden name was Califano. People think of me as being Hispanic, but I'm actually New York Italian. But, being married to Tony and so many of our friends being Hispanic, I took it as a second language. Plus, I learned to cook and fix Tony meals like his mother served when he was growing up." She gave a soft laugh to herself and continued, "Our friends and family call me Muncie."

I was stunned. It couldn't be possible. The coincidence was beyond comprehension. I swallowed hard, yet my mouth was dry. I placed the beer mug on a coaster and wiped my sweaty palms on my pant legs.

"Are you okay?" she asked as she scooted forward to the edge of the loveseat. "You look like you've seen a ghost."

Leaning forward, my eyes bore into hers. "Mrs. Castenada," I bumbled. Taking a deep breath, I allowed my heartbeat to slow.

"Mrs. Castenada...I'm sorry, Muncie." I paused to put my mind in order. "Muncie ..."

"Stop, Mr. Basurto, please. I apologize. I've upset you. What is it?" She was genuinely concerned.

I gave a half-hearted smile and sat back. "Mrs. Castenada, you had no way of knowing, and certainly I didn't. It's just that I've learned so much today, and when you said you were called Muncie..." I gave a self-deprecating chuckle, "I almost had a heart attack."

Fumbling for my wallet, I continued, "I want to show you my fiancé's picture." Pulling it out, I stepped around the table and handed the photograph to her. "Her name is Rosalinda Marquez, but I..."

Muncie Castenada's eyes froze on *my* Muncie's snapshot. "My God," she said. "She could pass for me twenty years ago."

I sat back down, took a long drink from the mug, and continued, "I've known Rosalinda and her family for years. We're going to be married this November."

"Congratulations are in order. Tell me about her," she said as she examined Rosalinda's picture.

"It's Muncie. That's her nickname. She's had it since high school." I was embarrassed, but shrugged and continued, "Muncie. It means rosy red cheeks, and it fits her to a 'T'."

Mrs. Castenada shook her head ever so slowly and studied the photo. "Ricky, I am so touched. My Tony nicknamed me for the very same reason, my red cheeks." She gave a little laugh and continued. "I was much younger, but oh, how Tony loved to tease me." She stopped, took a napkin from the table, and dabbed her eyes.

Tony Castenada and I had more in common than anything I had imagined.

* * *

We enjoyed casual family insights, drinking beer with chips and salsa until the sun went down in the west. Moving to the patio, we sat poolside and continued our exchange. She barely touched on her husband's murder, instead focusing on her immediate and extended families. She had no living relative from her side of the family. The Califanos were gone. In what struck me as bone-chilling, she told me her mother was shot and killed by teenage robbers when the family lived in New York City. Elizabeth, as she was known, was raised by a now-deceased grandparent in Florida. After high school, and as a bright and energetic teenager, the University of Arizona awarded her a scholarship to study Astronomy. It was on the sidewalk outside the AURA building where, by a fluke chance, she met the man of her dreams, Antonio Castenada.

Together, they had two sons, Matthew and Mark, both now grown men. Matthew followed in his mother's footsteps and worked at Kitt Peak Observatory. Mark joined the ROTC at the university and graduated with a degree in Public Administration. After graduation, he attended Officer Candidate School in Quantico, Virginia, and was stationed at Marine Corps Base, Camp Pendleton, California.

Her career didn't follow her college major but, after Tony's death, she became a dental hygienist and worked as such ever since then.

"Tony's family was generous," she commented. "We couldn't have made it without them but, between *them*, the financial support we received as a result of Tony's line-of-duty death and my paycheck, everything came together." She smiled when she looked up to the sky. The moon was cresting over the Rincon Mountains. "God was with us. We not only survived, but grew as a family."

A solitary tear dripped from her eye. Nodding her head, her words were as soft as velvet. "I know he's proud of us."

* * *

We talked until the moon was overhead. It was time to go. The house was dark and quiet when we walked toward the front, lit only by the waxing moon. I opened the door with her at my side. She touched my arm and a chill ran up the back of my neck. I turned. Our faces were only inches apart. She rose up on her toes and put her fingers to my face. The touch was as soft as angel's wings. Her lips brushed lightly against mine for the briefest moment.

She stepped back a few inches and looked into the depths of my soul. She held my hands and took a deep breath. Her lips quivered when she spoke. "I'll remember you always." Tears streamed down her cheeks. "Don't let your Muncie experience the evil that's waiting for you out there."

CHAPTER NINETEEN

S unrise greeted me when I crested Texas Canyon, eastbound on Interstate 10. The day was perfect. There wasn't a cloud in the sky. I glanced at my reflection in the mirror and smiled. Tucson was everything I had hoped for, and more. My questions had been answered. Mom's uncle, Detective Antonio Castenada, died as an honorable husband, father, and police officer. His legacy was more than simply having his name on a granite marker in the Memorial Plaza. His true gift to the world was the magnificent family he left behind—Muncie, Matthew, and Mark.

The taking of his life by the blood-sucking drug dealers was atrocious, but the personal accusations by the killers' defense team were beyond the scope of human decency. Yet, as Chief Hardyman had said, "In a way, justice had been done."

I found some satisfaction knowing Guzman and his lover paid with their lives, but nevertheless, couldn't completely accept the method by which it had been accomplished. I rationalized it by knowing their probable killer, Julian Espino Gatica, had paid the ultimate price for his unfathomable deeds. However, there was a degree of satisfaction that I had witnessed his final breath. If not for his torture of Sara Hurtado, Tony would not have been murdered.

Matagente received his just due.

I looked again in the mirror. *I haven't changed, have I?* I paused to consider it and concluded, *maybe so, maybe not.*

There was nothing to disturb my train of thought as I sped down the eastern slopes of Texas Canyon and onto the wide-open desolation of the Wilcox Salt Flats. Against my wishes, a scenario kept coming to the forefront of my consciousness. It was the *Yin* and *Yang* of recent weeks—the opposing and complementing principles of nature. Surely, Matagente and the 666 Mark of the Beast personified evil, and Guzman and his whore were comparably evil. Did the ends justify the means? I decided I didn't know, but might someday. Right now, the gas gauge showed near empty, but Wilcox was dead ahead.

I stopped at the Circle K for a fill-up, cold drink, and a visit to the restroom. Ten minutes later, I was back on the road with only two or three more hours to home.

Yin and Yang hung in the shadows of my mind, but at least were buried in the recesses of my psyche. I set the cruise control on 75 mph, pushed back in my seat and relaxed. Everything was good.

After a few miles, a highway sign caught my attention. It was like a shot between the eyes. I flicked off the cruise control and pulled onto the shoulder a mere dozen yards from the billboard. I couldn't breathe, but stared with that one-thousand-yard eye of a Marine sniper. Certainly, there must have been a similar posting for westbound traffic, but I had somehow missed it on my way to Tucson. But not today.

Historic Scenic Highway
Route 666
Next Exit

Yin and Yang controlled my body and soul. My heart pounded in my chest, my lips were parched, yet a cold sweat ran down my back. Was this my answer? I shook my head. *Not just no, but hell no.*

I flicked on my cellphone and looked up AZ Hwy. 666. Sure enough, it was there—a long history. I had no desire to learn if it was truly haunted. State government through the years had been pummeled with public demands to change the highway number due to the bizarre wrecks, ghost cars, faceless hitchhikers, and other unexplainable occurrences, so they changed its designator to Hwy. 491.

I didn't need a highway sign or anything else to tell me what I knew. Without a doubt, Julian Espino Gatica was Satan personified. I had seen his handiwork and needed no further evidence.

I shifted into drive and eased back into traffic, away from the narrow highway that bore the identifier of the Mark of the Beast. There was no need for the supposed Hounds of Hell chasing after me to prove the existence of evil. I had experienced it firsthand.

* * *

Rather than go directly to Columbus, I detoured south on Hwy. 146 to Hachita and our home site.

My heart sank when I reached the end of the dirt road to what had been our house. It was still a pile of ashes. The demolition and construction contracts had been signed, but nothing had been started. Lupe's and Rosalinda's words rang in my ears, "Ricky, you're too impatient. It'll take time."

I got out of my truck, walked around the debris mound to what had been my bedroom, now no more than a smelly pile of shit. I was angry and didn't give a damn about Yin and Yang. I knew what I knew. My mother had lost her house. Whatever we did to make her life whole again would always have a hole in it. She had been violated, and that would never go away.

Afterward, I sat in my truck, vented my anger, and let the tears flow. So much terror and destruction had come from our simple, uncomplicated arrests of two adults and a juvenile with fifty kilos of marijuana.

Was it worth it? We could argue that until the earth stood still.

I took a deep breath, dried my eyes, but couldn't control the thoughts raging through my mind. *We were young once…but not anymore.*

That was a 180-degree shift from where I was a few hours ago. What could change my mind in such a short time? Certainly not the highway sign or the destruction of our home. What could cause such a drastic mental turnaround? I thought of the aspen grove. Chop it down, burn it up. It doesn't make any difference. The roots are there, the grove will return, and so will the cartel. We destroyed a tunnel, arrested three people, and granted asylum to four adults and two children. So what?

Memories of the Castenada family threw me into psychological turmoil. Tony Castenada died fighting the drug dealers. So what? That was more than twenty years ago and the cartels had become stronger and more violent than ever before. *So why am I wasting my life on this so-called drug war?*

My answer, though, was clear. There was no alternative. It was the right thing to do. Pure and simple, like writing a straight line with crooked letters.

* * *

It was five o'clock by the time I reached *Las Haciendas de 9-11* in Columbus. Muncie was home, and the smell of an apple pie in the oven greeted me before my true love had a chance to kiss me.

During dinner, I told her about the Tucson trip: Chief Hardyman, Captain Willis, the photographer, and the Memorial Plaza. Equally important was what I didn't tell her—the role of retired CIA agent and Tucson Police detective Anthony Allbright.

After dinner, we went to the patio with a bottle of Pinot Grigio and two glasses. It was in that peaceful setting where I told her of Elizabeth Califano Castenada—Muncie, a rosy-cheeked college girl who encountered a stranger on campus at the University of Arizona and their lives together.

It was a sad but beautiful story. How a young mother with two little boys could not only face the world, but reach out to new heights with her faith, extended family, and the law enforcement community at her side. Little Elizabeth Califano, an orphan raised by an elderly grandmother, took on the world and won. And so did my mother, Sophie Diaz Basurto.

The moon was full when we emptied the last drop of wine, held each other's hands, and strolled in silence to our apartment. It had been a good day.

* * *

I woke at the first cooing of the dove. Muncie was still asleep, so I showered, shaved, and was at the office by six o'clock. My first surprise was to find O'Rourke's vehicle there, especially on a Saturday.

I grabbed a quick cup of sludge coffee from the vending machine, then went directly to Miguel's office. He looked up, startled when I knocked on the doorframe and spoke, "What's up, Boss? It's Saturday. You're supposed to be off."

He leaned back in his chair, nursing his coffee while he looked over the rim of the cup at me. "Basurto, you're back. I figured you'd be gone all weekend."

I pulled up a chair and sat across from him, sipping my coffee. I nodded my head, smiled, and spit out my notes like the narrative of a crime report. "Everything I'd hoped for and more. Antonio Castenada was my mother's uncle. He was killed in a police parking garage, most likely by a cartel boss' lover, Mary Elizabeth Martin. One shot to the head with a .38. Neither she nor anyone else was ever charged with his murder.

"Our bad guy, Matagente, was the person who tortured a female confidential informant, and that's what led to Tony Castenada being fingered as a cop." I shook my head, "But every one of them walked—no charges at all. Except, Guzman and Martin each took a .22 to the back of the head, most likely from Matagente." I shrugged. "And you know what happened to him." I gave a deep exhale of resignation. "Case closed."

O'Rourke was in such a good mood that he made another pot of coffee in his Mister Coffee and we each had a fresh cup. We continued our conversation, or more like my monologue, about the Tucson Police Department, the memorial, and Mrs. Castenada. We talked about everything except my private visit with Anthony Allbright. Some things were better left unsaid.

After we had drained his coffee pot, he put his cup down and spoke. "I'm glad you're back and more than glad about how things went. Now, though, I'll bring you up to speed on what's been happening here." Reaching into his desk drawer, he pulled out his iPad.

"Let me show you some statistics from the last few days, and what it means for us, the whole team. Antelope Wells normally had about a couple of dozen legal border crossers each day. Now they are receiving up to two thousand per day, most of them seeking asylum. Columbus and Santa Teresa border crossings both have skyrocketed." He looked up from the computer screen and looked into my eyes. "Do you know what this means?"

I nodded. "I think so. Border Patrol and Customs are swamped, so we have everything else."

He chuckled. "You're a smart guy, Ricky. With everyone else running around with illegals looking for asylum, getting into the country to have their children, plus Border Patrol taking on feeding and burping babies, you, me, and the rest of our team are all that's left to take on the narcotraffickers, and, get *this*...junior narcotraffickers."

"The what?"

"They're teaching their kids how to run dope and shoot guys like us." He frowned and gave a grim chuckle. "Yeah, what do you think about that?"

I paused and considered the truth of the growing challenge that confronted us. It was devastating. I looked directly at Supervisory Agent Miguel O'Rourke and gave him a simple response, "It makes me think about the aspen groves."

Puzzled by my reply, he tilted his head like a puppy hearing a distant siren. "What?"

EPILOGUE

The Salinas Family

The Crime Laboratory and the Intelligence Fusion Centers failed to establish prosecutable evidence against Rodrigo Nicolas Salinas or his sons, Alberto and Federico. They remain in intelligence files as "Persons of Interest" for drug and/or human trafficking.

The Gonzales Family

The six members of the Gonzales family were granted asylum. The grandparents, Abel and Elise, remained as full-time employees of the Montenegro Agriculture Complex. Emilio, Abril, and Felix live in Alamogordo, New Mexico. Their daughter, Catalina, remains in a local mental health facility, but occasionally is granted a weekend pass to be with her family.

Emilio and Abril have minimum wage but full-time employment and benefits at DynCorp, a supply company serving Holloman Air Force Base.

Felix is a student at Sierra Blanca Middle School and is on the cross-country team.

Sophie Basurto

The construction of her home was completed in October. She lives alone, has a new chicken coop, and a dozen hens. She adopted a shepherd mixed breed dog she found wandering the near-ghost town of Hachita. The dog's name is *Duro*, because he had to be a tough little s.o.b. to survive out there.

Her home was furnished as a gift from an anonymous donor who she suspected was her son's new father-in-law. Mrs. Basurto is a full-time retiree, serving as a volunteer at the Animas Pre-School three days per week. She no longer takes in laundry.

Enrique and Rosalinda

Mr. and Mrs. Ricky Basurto were married in San Albino Cathedral on November 30th. Included in their guest list were Elizabeth Castenada and her sons, Matthew and Mark.

At the behest of powerful and wealthy donors in Chihuahua, the Mexican government declared Enrique as *Persona non Grata,* denying him legal entry into Mexico.

He continued service with the New Mexico State Police, attached to the Human and Drug Trafficking Task Force serving the NM Highways 9 and 11 area of southern New Mexico.

One year to the day after their marriage, Muncie gave birth to their daughter, Guadalupe Elizabeth Basurto. The child's godmother was Elizabeth Castenada.

Rosalinda Basurto continued her employment with New Mexico State University.

The Aspen Grove

The beautiful mountain groves and the brutal cartels continue to grow unabated.

El Fin

Made in the USA
Coppell, TX
26 August 2022

8199092 7R00085